The May Day Mystery

Introduction

There is no Port Trepoldern in Cornwall, England, but it is meant to be rather like Padstow. I hope the people of Padstow will forgive me for describing a May Day Festival that is, in many ways, very like their own, though they have two "horses" and Port Trepoldern has only one . . . the Great Horse.

The words of the Trepoldern song are my own, but I hope they have the true "folk" atmosphere. So often these ancient songs contain words that have been corrupted down through the ages so that the original meaning is lost, and they often mention long forgotten people.

The "hobby-horse" is known in other parts of England, including Minehead in Devon, but the "hoss" varies much in appearance. Sometimes the whole upper part of a man's body is visible; at Padstow, and in my story, he is almost completely hidden under the heavy frame. The tall pointed mask at Padstow is thought to indicate

The May Day Mystery

by

Mabel Esther Allan

Criterion Books
New York

By Mabel Esther Allan

THE BALLET FAMILY
THE DANCING GARLANDS: THE BALLET FAMILY AGAIN
THE MYSTERY BEGAN IN MADEIRA
MYSTERY OF THE SKI SLOPES
MYSTERY ON THE FOURTEENTH FLOOR
THE SIGN OF THE UNICORN
SIGNPOST TO SWITZERLAND
THE KRAYMER MYSTERY

Library of Congress Catalog Card No.: 70-134561
Standard Book Number: 0.200.71789.8
Copyright © 1971 by Mabel Esther Allan
Printed in the United States of America

Criterion Books

An Intext Publisher

that originally a unicorn was worshipped.

In the mists of history different animal gods were venerated all over the world, but it is always something of a miracle to find such a survival in a little English town. And the strange, eerie atmosphere remains, especially when the "hoss" goes through the dying ceremony and most people sink down with it onto the old cobblestones.

The death of winter and the rebirth of spring . . . that was the basic meaning. And when the horse rises again and dances on, the music is joyous and everyone follows, singing. Today, maybe people don't feel the primitive fervor of remote man, to whom the awakening earth was all important. But something remains here and there in remote places to remind us that our history stretches back and back into an almost unimaginable distance.

Mabel Esther Allan

1. The Invitation

Until that particular Friday in April Laura Edmund had never heard of the Trepoldern horse. She knew of Elvan's existence, because she had seen his photograph in Rose's room, but it had never crossed her mind that she would ever meet him.

It was raining hard and bitterly cold as she approached the house off Fulham Road, where she had lived for some months, and she was deeply sunk into depression. She tried to tell herself that this was a shameful mood, quite unsuited to a girl who had fought hard for independence.... for the right to live and work in London.

She had never admitted to anyone, scarcely even to herself, that she was still terribly homesick. Six months in London had made her a different girl from the shy but determined eighteen-year-old who had left the North. On the surface she was confident, efficient and well able to cope with her job in a City bank, with rush hour crowds and all the other aspects of her life. Yet there were times when she was dreadfully lonely, and the problem of what to do with her coming vacation was getting her down.

She really did love London and now knew it quite well. She had friends and even a boy friend, who worked with her at the bank. But now she wanted a real change; the country.

In the early days she had sometimes been teased. "So you're from the darkest North?" In fact, she came from Cheshire, from the Wirral Peninsula, and it wasn't "dark" at all. She had lived in a charming modern house on the Dee marshes, with views over the River Dee to the hills of Wales. The sound of seabirds ... the highest tides creeping over the marsh grass ... heavenly sunsets.

And she had exchanged all this for a life of independence, for a room in a tall, rather grim London house. For suppers cooked on a gas ring when she wasn't going out.

London was beautiful in April when it wasn't raining so hard. There was blossom in the parks and the leaves were a sharp, heart-stirring green, but she longed inexpressibly for the country. And the whole trouble was that she couldn't go home, for the Wirral house had been rented furnished in March and her parents had gone to Kenya for six months.

"I hate leaving you behind in England," her mother had said. "But I know you love your job and the aunts will keep in close touch with you. You can go to Birmingham for the weekend whenever you like, and Aunt Elsa will love to have you in Glasgow for your holidays."

Laura only knew, as she let herself into the rather

dismal, brown-painted hall, that she didn't want to go to either Birmingham or Glasgow. She hadn't even told the aunts that she was having to take her vacation early. But what *else* was there to do?

There was a blue airmail letter on the hall table, and, at the sight of it, all Laura's unreasonable misery surged up in a wave. Oh, why had her father had to go so far away on business? Why hadn't she begged to be allowed to go with them? Well, pride, of course. They would have taken her gladly, but she had always painted her new life in such glowing colors that they had believed she wouldn't wish to go.

Holding her mother's letter, she began to climb the stairs. The first flight was wide and had once been quite elegant. Her room was under the roof; a big attic that had at first seemed quite romantic. Her first home in London. Now she dreaded the rest of the lonely evening.

As she started up the second flight, self-pity really gripped her and she stopped, pushing back her red hair and blinking away tears.

Footsteps above . . . someone coming toward her.

"Oh, hullo! Is something the matter, Laura?" Rose Tregarth's voice, lilting and deep.

Laura took out her handkerchief and mopped fiercely at her eyes. Rose lived on the floor below her. They had known each other slightly for nearly six months, but had never shown any signs of growing close. Rose was nearly nineteen; a handsome, dark girl, a little remote in manner. She worked in an office in

Kingsway and she came from Cornwall, which accounted for her lovely voice. Laura had always thought that Rose was unhappy, but there had been no confidences on either side. Over occasional cups of coffee in Rose's room they had talked about the theatre, books and life in London. Two exiles, it seemed, but each had her pride.

"It's nothing," said Laura, and gulped, glad that the stairs were dark.

"It must be something, my dear. I saw there was a letter for you. Not bad news, I hope?"

Rose must be going out. Laura was late home because she had stayed in the City to have coffee and sandwiches with Geoffrey. He was going to night school, to his French class. Geoffrey wanted to improve himself and maybe work in another country. He found the bank dull.

"I haven't even read the letter yet. It's nothing, honestly. I'm just being a baby; I'm so ashamed. It's a beastly evening and I—well, I just got miserable. You must be in a hurry."

"No," said Rose. "I just thought I'd go to the cinema, but I'm not set on it. Come up to my room. You're wet and cold."

Laura went. She had always been attracted to Rose Tregarth and had wished, vaguely, that they were better friends. It would have been interesting if Rose would talk about Cornwall. Laura had been there twice and loved it.

Rose's room was very neat. There were photographs

on the shelf over her books. Her father and mother, she had said once, and her brothers and sister. Elvan was the elder brother. He looked about twenty-two and had a Puckish face, with thick dark eyebrows and springing dark hair. A strange name, Elvan! Laura had always wished she knew more about him, but Rose never said much about her family.

"Sit on the bed and I'll heat up some coffee," Rose said briskly. "I've had mine, but you look. . . . Would you like some scrambled eggs or something?"

"No, I've had something to eat, but coffee would be lovely," Laura said, still a little shakily. "It's terribly nice of you! I thought I was grown up and sensible."

Rose glanced at the pale, downbent face. Laura's long lashes hid her hazel eyes. Her mouth was sensitive and the whole attractive face was not particularly "sensible."

"You may as well tell me. You just got miserable, you said. Did you quarrel with Geoffrey?"

"No. Oh, no. I don't quarrel with Geoffrey. I don't think I care enough," Laura confessed. "It was just—" Well, it was a little late for pride after she had revealed so much. She explained in a burst of words. How she was sometimes lonely and homesick, and how much, in spite of liking London, she longed for the country. And now there was her coming vacation, starting in a week's time, and she didn't want to go to stay with either aunt.

Rose listened gravely.

"Isn't there anything else you could do?" she asked.

"I can't think of anything. I wouldn't enjoy it if I went

somewhere alone, and I suppose I'd have to tell the aunts and they'd fuss. They feel responsible for me. In fact, Aunt Elsa thought it was awful to let me come to London alone. And I don't know anyone who is having their vacation at the same time. It's so early—"

"Then you'd better come home with me," said Rose.

Laura jumped and nearly spilled her coffee.

"With *you?* You can't mean it! To Cornwall?" To Cornwall . . . that rather mysterious county that was, in some ways, as foreign as Wales. Almost cut off from the rest of England by the River Tamar, and once with its own language. To meet the brother with the interesting eyebrows and the intelligent, humorous face, and the little brother and sister. It was a great surprise, as Rose had scarcely mentioned her home.

"Yes, of course to Cornwall, my dear." She said "my dear" in a way that Laura had only ever heard in Cornwall. "You see, I'm taking my vacation at the end of next week and going West on Saturday."

"It's—it's awfully nice of you! But wouldn't your mother mind? Hadn't you better ask her?"

"I will, of course," said Rose calmly. "And you had better explain to your aunts. Mother always said to bring any friends I liked. We're a very friendly family and you said you liked Cornwall. Didn't you stay at Marazion once?"

"Yes, and another time at Sennen. I loved it all. Not only the coast, but some of that queer, bleak inland country. Abandoned tin mines, and standing stones, and earthen banks instead of hedges. I don't even know where you live," Laura added.

"At Trepoldern. Port Trepoldern. It's a fishing village —well, a small town, really—on the north coast, a few miles from Newquay." Rose paused and then said in a strained voice, "I haven't been home for almost a year. I didn't even go at Christmas. I stayed with a married cousin in Surrey. There really wasn't time to go so far, or that's what I said. But I *have* to be there for May Day. I can't miss that!"

"May Day?" Laura repeated stupidly. So Rose *had* been unhappy; there had obviously been some reason why she had stayed away from Cornwall for so long. But why May Day should draw her home at last was completely puzzling.

"And you ought to see it," Rose went on, "if you never have. Our May Day festival. The Festival of the Great Horse, we call it. The Trepoldern hoss. Like Padstow, you know, in some ways. We like to think ours is older, but they both go back into the mists of history. Prehistory. My father will tell you all about it. He's a Cornish authority, and he also knows a lot about these strange old survivals in different parts of the world. He farms a bit and writes books in his spare time. Did you never notice those?"

Laura stared at the bottom shelf of the bookcase. She usually looked at people's books, but somehow she had never liked to show curiosity in Rose's room.

"No. *Old Cornish Customs. Animal Gods in Europe.*

Is George Tregarth your father, then? He must be very clever."

"Yes," Rose agreed. "He's quite a character, my father."

"But I don't understand about May Day. It sounds fascinating!" Laura was warm and very much happier. Her state of depression now seemed absurd.

"You will. You'll sing the song at midnight and all day on May Day, and you'll follow the Great Horse. They say the song draws Trepoldern people back across the world, and it's certainly drawing me back from London," Rose said somberly. "Have some more coffee?"

"No, thank you. Did you *have* to stay away?" Laura ventured. It seemed like a violation of their cautious friendship, but if she was really going to Trepoldern surely she had better understand.

"I thought I had. Oh, for months I didn't want to talk about it. I was in love," Rose explained quickly. "I'd loved him since I was a child. His name is Peter Poldern. I was thirteen when I first knew how I felt, and he was eighteen. Of course he never guessed how I felt. No one knew, unless my mother had some idea. She's very perceptive. It just grew stronger and stronger and he just went on treating me like a child. A child he liked very much. He and his parents have always been family friends. Then quite suddenly, fifteen months ago, he decided that he wanted a change of scene and he went off to work in Canada. They have relatives there, with a big farm in Alberta, and he loves the land and an outdoor life."

14   The May Day Mystery

Laura sat and stared at her. It must be dreadful to love someone who was thousands of miles away and quite unknowing.

"But. . . . You're going back. Have you got over it, then?"

"No. I just can't forget him. But I realized suddenly that I can't stay away from home forever. And, even though last May Day was so terrible, it's always been part of my life. It nearly killed me when he went," Rose confessed. "I just wanted to die, and it was worst on May Day. The music going on and on and the horse dancing through the streets. Everyone laughing and singing and me trying not to cry. Every time the horse 'died' I felt I might die, too. That was when I decided I had to leave right away. Father wasn't keen, but I think Mother persuaded him to let me go."

"Oh, dear! But it may still be awful this time."

"It can't be as bad as last year," Rose said grimly. "And I do love it. I was introduced to the horse when I was just a tiny baby. All the children are. You'll understand when you see it. You will come?"

"Of course, if you're sure you really want me. I do so long for real air and the smell of the sea," Laura said fervently.

She said goodbye soon afterward and climbed the stairs to her room; now she had plenty to occupy her mind. Rose and her hopeless, romantic love and all that strange talk about the Great Horse. It didn't seem to be a real horse. A hobby-horse, wasn't that the term? She had always loved old things and ancient tunes. And how exciting to be going to meet all the Tregarths! It would be wonderful to cross the Tamar into Cornwall again.

On Tuesday Rose told Laura that her mother was delighted that they were both arriving on the weekend. What with the nearness of May Day, and the thought of seeing their sister again, Mrs. Tregarth wrote, Lellie and Isaac were so excited they were nearly driving the rest of them mad.

"What very strange names you have in your family," Laura remarked.

"Oh, Lellie is Lelant and Isaac is a place name, too, in this case. Port Isaac, you know. So is Elvan. There was a Cornish saint called St. Elvan." Once started on talking about her home and family, Rose had grown articulate and could hardly stop. Laura didn't want her to. "I'm Rosemullion, really."

"Goodness! But it's very pretty!"

"Mother says she lost her head a bit with some of us. When Elvan was born she'd just read a book in which all the characters were called after Cornish place names. There are a lot of attractive ones. Rosemullion is a headland, but people would laugh if I used it all."

"Oh, I'm so glad I'm coming with you! Aunt Elsa was quite nice about it when I telephoned."

Laura thought she had never seen Rose look so animated. Peter Poldern must have been blind not to see how good-looking she was. Not pretty exactly, but striking, with lovely coloring. Even at thirteen she must have been worth looking at. Yet he had gone off to

Canada without a word. Perhaps he had known her too well and thought of her more as a sister or cousin.

On Friday, when Laura returned from work, Rose met her on the landing. She held a letter and was frowning.

"What's the matter?" Laura asked sharply. How dreadful if the trip to Cornwall was off!

"Nothing really. It's just rather strange and worrying. Come in."

"Can't we go?"

"Oh, of course. But there was some kind of intruder a couple of nights ago, and Joseph, an old man who works for us, was hurt. He seems to have gone out to investigate and was hit on the head."

"How awful! Someone in the garden, do you mean?"

"In the—no, I won't explain. I want it to be a surprise," Rose said. "Joseph's in hospital and it's a complete mystery who was there and what he was after. Trepoldern's such a quiet little place. There's hardly ever any kind of crime. Just an occasional quarrel and fight, or someone drunk and disorderly. There was a murder once, but that was about twenty years ago."

"Goodness! Who was murdered?"

"An old servant in that case, and there was a theft as well. But the whole thing was never solved. It's a mystery to this day. We were all brought up on the story. You'll hear it when you get to Trepoldern."

"But if your mother's upset, perhaps I oughtn't to go with you," Laura said slowly.

"Don't be silly! It's not as serious as that; just rather puzzling and worrying."

"I didn't expect a mystery as well as all the rest."

"Oh, it was probably some silly kid. We have a few in Trepoldern, the same as most places. We'd better pack."

Laura went off to her room and pulled out the old suitcase that held some of her country clothes and shoes. London clothes wouldn't be much use in Cornwall. Slacks, she'd need; and plenty of warm sweaters, and one or two pretty dresses in case they went out in the evening.

Trepoldern sounded more and more interesting and there was a lot to learn. That old mystery, whatever it was, and Rose's suggestion that her home was unusual in some way.

She could hardly wait for the next day!

2. A Surprise for Laura

The Cornish Riviera Express was very crowded. There were a great many sailors returning to Plymouth and Devonport, and it was hard to find room for all Rose's parcels and packages. She had presents for her whole family, and the most awkward one of all was a model of the Tower of London for Isaac. However, a young man wedged it on top of his kitbag and they settled down.

Laura was silent with excitement. By late afternoon she would have seen the Tregarths' house and met the family. May Day was still several days away, but her curiosity about the horse was enormous. And even the thought of seeing Cornwall again—of walking by the sea and exploring the old fishing port—was thrilling. The whole thing still seemed to her a kind of miracle.

Rose, too, was quiet as the train gathered speed. She stared through the window at the environs of London. Her face was grave and Laura's heart warmed in sympathy. Rose was going back to where she belonged, but Peter Poldern wouldn't be there.

Rose, after a time, seemed so remote and unapproachable again that Laura began to feel uneasy. Perhaps she was regretting taking a friend. And no one could say they had actually been friends until the last week. Yet she liked Rose and felt sure they'd get on well.

They went to have lunch early, and when they were settled at a table, Laura said:

"I do wish you'd tell me about your house. Or is it a farm?"

Rose came back from a great distance. She had been thinking of a day when she was sixteen and Peter had taken her fishing.

"It's a house. The farm is half a mile away. You'll see in a few hours. You'll like it, I promise you."

"Is it near the sea?"

"It looks down on the harbor. Of course Port Trepoldern isn't much of a fishing port any more. None of them are. There isn't much work. People are poor, very often. There are Trepoldern people all over the world. During the past twenty-five years or so, several groups have gone to Australia. I always think it's sad they can't make a living in their native place."

"Did you see that lot?" Laura asked suddenly.

"No." Rose had been looking out of the window as she talked.

"They just passed through, carrying bottles of beer or something. Some of those long-haired types . . . such peculiar clothes, and pretty dirty. Beatniks. . . . Hippies. I heard one of them mention Trepoldern."

Rose groaned.

"They're early, but I suppose they're going for May Day. There were some last year. The Festival seems to fascinate them. The local people hate having them around."

The train sped on westward, and as they approached Plymouth, Laura's excitement increased. Soon now over the River Tamar into Cornwall!

Crowds left the train at Plymouth and they had the compartment to themselves.

"Now it's terribly slow," said Rose. "Stopping at several little stations."

"Are you wishing you hadn't come?" Laura asked tentatively.

"No, not really. I've missed it so much. But I *am* a little scared. Some things are sure to be different. Lellie and Isaac are a whole year older; perhaps we'll hardly know each other. And people have got married or died. Mother's told me most of the news in her letters, of course. In her last letter she told me that the Vicar's grandson has come back from Australia and apparently the old people are very thrilled. The Vicar is seventy-five and his wife is an invalid. I've known them all my life. Actually they're both growing rather tiresome. The Vicar always was a rather stuffy and conventional kind of man and he isn't very popular. Perhaps having a young man around will wake them up."

"Had he been in Australia long?" Laura asked.

"Oh, he was born there. His grandparents had never seen him. Their only son, Arthur, went to Australia a long time ago and married there. He and his wife died in an accident and little Arthur was adopted by his mother's mother. I think the Vicar and his wife more or less lost touch then."

"Oh!" This was another romantic story. "And now he's back?"

"Yes, he'd just arrived when Mother wrote. It's quite a nine days' wonder. You'll meet him, of course."

Then they saw the wide, shining waters of the Tamar and were crossing the bridge into Cornwall. After a cloudy morning the sun had come out brilliantly, and in East Cornwall the banks were thick with primroses and the trees were a delicate green.

They were leaving the train at Par, where Rose's father was to meet them. And, before Laura expected it, they were almost there. She began to feel shy and a little scared. A strange family . . . a man who wrote books. Elvan! It would be odd to meet him after knowing his photograph. She knew she was predisposed to like him.

"You'll like Elvan," said Rose, almost as if she had read Laura's thoughts. And then she added, with perhaps less tact than might have been expected from her, "Girls have always liked Elvan. We used to tease him dreadfully."

"Really?" Laura immediately vowed that if she liked him she would keep it to herself. "Is he engaged?"

Rose frowned.

"I don't think so. Not actually engaged. Mother did mention some girl at the place where he works. Elvan has a good job. I expect he'll want to marry soon." Then she leaped up and began to assemble their cases and all the packages by the door. She was white and brilliant-eyed.

A man came along the corridor and stood just behind them. Rose said something about being in Trepoldern in about thirty minutes and the man asked:

"You two young ladies are going to Trepoldern? Now perhaps you can tell me about the bus—"

"Oh, there's sure to be one to meet this train," Rose told him.

"Well, that's splendid, just splendid!" he said, in a rather fussy voice. "You're visitors, perhaps? Going to Trepoldern for May Day?"

Rose glanced at him vaguely. He was elderly and very shabby. He wore an old, stained raincoat and his grey hair was too long and rather wild. He had a grey moustache and a little beard, and he held what looked like a tape recorder in one hand. A battered suitcase stood beside him.

"No," said Rose, as the train stopped. "I live there."

"But how very interesting! I'm delighted to meet a resident of such a very interesting place. I'm a folklorist and—"

Rose opened the door and jumped out. Laura handed down the cases and packages and the shabby man followed them. He hesitated a moment and walked to the exit.

Rose and Laura were slower, because they had so much to carry and they got involved with the crowd of long-haired young men. They certainly were bizarre and dirty. Usual enough in London, but out of place on a country station.

"Sorry, dear!" said one wearing a violent purple sweater and green trousers. He had nearly knocked one of Rose's parcels out of her arms with his roll of what appeared to be bedding. He also carried a huge rucksack.

The strangers climbed into the green bus that was waiting, and Rose looked around in dismay.

"I wonder where Father is!"

There had been a few cars drawn up outside the station, but now they had picked up their passengers and gone.

"I expect he'll be here in a minute," said Laura, who was glad of the respite. She stood there, breathing the sweet air, listening to birdsong.

The Trepoldern bus departed and they were the only ones left outside the station. Five minutes passed and then a very large, very shabby car came sweeping toward them, drawing up with a flourish. There was a dark-haired young man wearing a duffle coat at the wheel.

"It's Elvan!" cried Rose, and ran forward.

Elvan got out and kissed his sister briefly.

"Well, Rose, my dear! It's good to see you again. How we've all missed you. I'm sorry I'm late. Father got held up at the farm, so I said I'd come. Is this all your stuff? And—" His dark eyes gazed at Laura, who blushed because she had been staring. He was very like his photograph, but his coloring made him even more handsome than she had expected.

"This is my brother Elvan, Laura," Rose said quickly. "Laura Edmund. Yes, I think this is the lot, unless we left anything on the train. Do take care of the Tower of London. It's so clever; really detailed. I thought Isaac would like it. And this is Mother's hat."

"The hat and the Tower can go on top of the rest," said Elvan, starting to stow everything in the back of the car. "You seem to have brought plenty, my dear," he added.

"Presents for everyone," said Rose. She stood beside the car, breathing deeply. "Oh, how lovely it smells! Not like London. Is there room for us both in front?"

"Just about. Do you know Cornwall?" the young man asked Laura, smiling at her appreciatively. She looked very attractive, with her red hair blowing gently and her eager, bemused expression.

"A little. I've been twice. It's very kind of you all to—"

"Oh, we were delighted—a friend of Rose!"

He drove away, rather too fast. The Tower of London slid off the pile at the back and Rose wailed.

Elvan seemed to concentrate on his driving at first and didn't speak much. The roads were narrow and winding, here and there deeply wooded. Then they were in bleaker country, though it was brightened by the golden flare of the gorse and primroses on the earthen banks. There was less traffic and Laura saw the long brown hands relax on the wheel.

As they came down off a ridge into a river valley, Elvan Tregarth said:

"So May Day brought you back, Rose?"

"That and—well, I had to come home," Rose answered.

"Of course you had. London isn't the place for you. And you've come at the right time. I have some news for you," said Elvan, and his voice changed. "We heard this afternoon. Peter Poldern is coming home for May Day."

Laura had the impression that the car lurched, but perhaps that was only because she felt Rose go rigid beside her.

"Coming back? From Canada?"

"Yes." His eyes were on the road, but Laura was sure he knew how his sister felt. "I gather it was a sudden decision. He's flying to London tomorrow and hopes to arrive here on Monday. His people are delighted, of course, and it will be good to see old Peter again."

"Yes, very good," said Rose, in a breathless voice. She was gripping her lower lip with her teeth.

"This is the River Poldern," Elvan said, apparently to Laura. "Five miles now. You must be dying for a cup of tea. I have to collect something in the town, but it won't take a moment."

They passed the green bus, which seemed to have made good speed. Laura caught a glimpse of the folklorist's straggly grey hair and drew Rose's attention to him.

"He seemed an awful old man!" said Rose, making a

great effort to sound normal. "A folklorist! Well, he won't be very popular in Trepoldern. We like to keep our May Day Festival to ourselves. Of course, some visitors do come, but we hate publicity. The B.B.C. came last year, but no one was keen about it." Then she changed the subject. "How's Joseph, Elvan?"

"Oh, doing fine. That's why I was late. I looked into the hospital and he talked so much I couldn't get away. He'll be home in a day or two. Lucky he has such a thick skull!"

They passed a notice that said "Port Trepoldern" and went more slowly down into the town. The hill was lined with flat-fronted grey cottages, and then the winding streets were very narrow.

"Small, but picturesque," said Elvan. "At least, so visitors seem to think."

The place seemed asleep. Granite cottages, little shops, even narrower streets, then they passed an old inn and were out by the harbor.

Laura gave a cry of pleasure. The water was blue, there were gaily painted boats, and high on a cliff on the right were the ruins of a castle.

"Oh, it's lovely!" she cried.

Elvan stopped the car and jumped out. He disappeared into a little store on the quay, and then Rose put out her hand and briefly took Laura's.

"It can't be true, can it? Peter coming back?"

"It seems to be true," said Laura cautiously.

"For May Day. . . . Did the tune do that to him, too? Oh, I just can't believe it!"

A Surprise for Laura   27

As they sat there the bus arrived and disgorged about a dozen people. The motley crowd from London, the folklorist, and a few who were clearly Trepoldern people, for they greeted three old fishermen who were sitting on a bench.

The folklorist glanced around him and then approached the car.

"We meet again!" he said to Laura, who was nearest the open window. "How very delightful! I'm looking for the Ship Inn. That one we passed, I observed, was the Blue Boat."

"Oh, we have plenty of inns," said Rose. "But most of them don't take visitors. The Ship is around the harbor. If you just go that way you'll see it."

"I thank you. We'll meet again, I have no doubt, and perhaps you can tell me—"

Elvan came back, carrying a large box, which he stowed in the boot. The old man, not finishing his sentence, picked up his shabby suitcase and walked away.

"Was that your folklorist?" he asked, as he took the wheel again. "Quite a character, I should think."

"Mad as a hatter!" said Rose uncharitably.

Elvan drove away through the winding streets and soon they were climbing, though not up the hill down which they had come. The last grey cottage was passed and the view of the river opened out. Laura looked ahead at the frowning ruins of the castle. There was no house in sight up on the cliff.

The road turned into a track and they bumped a good deal. There was valerian on the banks, already in bud.

When they turned a corner Laura looked down on the grey roofs of the little town, and she wondered how it was possible that the place should hold a prehistoric thing like the Festival of the Great Horse.

The ruined walls of the castle were very near. With a swoop and an increase of speed Elvan shot the car up the last steep rise, and they drove through a gap where there might once have been great gates and stopped in a grassy courtyard.

"Oh, you might have told me you lived in such a wonderful place!" Laura gasped, looking around. "Why, I should have seen the house over the walls from below."

"It doesn't show much unless you know it's there," Rose said, looking pleased. "I wanted it to be a surprise."

"It certainly is!"

There was really very little of the castle left; just the outer walls and a ruined tower. But within the shelter of the walls—nothing like so old, perhaps only two hundred years—was a solid stone house. It was not elegant or beautiful, but its romantic setting gave it an instant appeal. The gulls screamed around the tower, and through gaps in the walls Laura could see the river and the shining sea, both blue in the bright afternoon light.

In fact, after the house near the Fulham Road, it was almost too much . . . purest romance. A castle in Cornwall! No wonder Rose had had to come home!

3. Dinner at Poldern Place

Elvan got out of the car and walked around to open the door by Laura. He looked amused.

"Didn't Rose tell you? Trepoldern Castle. It was a little caught up in the Arthurian legend, though of course Tintagel is better known and has a more dramatic setting. The Poldern family used to own it. They've been here since the Dark Ages. One of their ancestors built the house in 1763. My father bought the whole property quite cheaply more than twenty years ago."

"So the Polderns are an important family? I didn't realize that." Laura was out in the sun, enjoying the smell of grass and earth and the sea.

"Lords of the Manor. They're pretty poor nowadays, though. That's Poldern Place on the hill the other side of the town." He took Laura's arm, led her to one of the gaps in the wall, and pointed out the long, low grey house. There was a tower apparently joined to it on the north side, and the whole was backed by trees.

The firmness of his touch startled Laura into an awareness she had never felt before in her life. He was a tall young man and looked strong. After nearly six months of knowing his photograph it was strange to see his face in reality.

Laura heard excited voices, and when she turned, the courtyard seemed full of people and animals. Though actually, there were only three adults and two children and it was the two leaping dogs and three cats that lent real movement to the scene. The ginger cat, affected by the excitement, leaped on to the little boy's shoulder and perched there, waving a red-gold tail.

Rose stood in the middle of it all, like a bewitched princess in a ballet. A fanciful idea, Laura thought wryly, but anyone would be fanciful in such a setting. It was really more like a dream than a ballet.

And then Rose called her over and introduced her to her father and mother, the old woman called Bess who looked after them all, and the little dark-haired girl and boy. Lelant was eleven and very pretty, and Isaac, nine, was very like his older brother.

"We're so pleased to meet you, Laura," Mrs. Tregarth said. "We always told Rose to bring any of her friends from London." She had untidy brown hair, a pale face and very beautiful eyes, and wore no makeup; she was dressed in an old red sweater and slacks.

Laura felt terribly shy, though they all seemed so friendly. She was shyest of all of Rose's father. He was tall, with grizzled hair and he was dressed like a farmer. But his intelligent face made her remember those books on Rose's shelf. He was an author, a real author. She had never met one before.

"Tea's ready," said Mrs. Tregarth. "Let the girls get

indoors, children. They must be tired after their journey. I'll show Laura to her room."

Laura found herself detached from the rest of them and led across a shabbily furnished but charming hall, and up the stairs.

"The spare room has the nicest view in the whole house," Mrs. Tregarth told her, opening a door. "Look! You can see over the lowest part of the walls."

"It's wonderful!" Laura cried. She could see the harbor and the whole little town outspread, and beyond the opposite cliff to where the river opened out into the shining sea. A little to her right was the ruined tower of the old castle, with valerian growing between the stones.

"Well, unpack later. The bathroom is the second door on the left. Rose's room is next to yours on the other side."

Laura washed hastily and returned to her room to powder her nose and run a comb through her hair. She had not quite closed the door and suddenly she heard Rose's voice:

"Oh, Mother, it is good to be back. I'm sorry I stayed away for so long."

Mrs. Tregarth's voice was quieter, but still audible:

"I understood, my dear, but I knew you didn't want to talk about it."

"And now he's coming home," said Rose.

"Yes, and I only hope it doesn't mean more sorrow for you."

"Just to see him—"

"Oh, dear!" Mrs. Tregarth sounded dismayed. "Rose, perhaps he isn't worth it. Oh, what's the good of saying that, when you're so much in love." Then she went on, more lightly: "Elvan's taking some of his vacation. Did he tell you? He says he needs some air. I suppose he'll get more fishing; he does enjoy it. He and Arthur Pengwern have been out once or twice in the evenings."

"The Vicar's grandson? What is he like?"

"We-ell," Mrs. Tregarth hesitated. "It isn't fair to judge. He's rather alien, having lived in Australia all his life. Quite a good-looking young man, and extremely friendly, but rather—well, I'm afraid the only word for it is 'brash'."

"He doesn't sound like Elvan's kind of person," Rose remarked.

"No, but the Vicar asked him to be friendly. He's so afraid Arthur will be bored in Trepoldern. Mrs. Pengwern has taken a real fancy to him, it seems. Of course it's natural enough, as he's their only grandson. They want him to settle here, but somehow I don't feel he will."

Then Laura was ready and she coughed a little as she opened her door, to warn them. They were standing just inside Rose's room, with the door wide open.

"Tea!" said Mrs. Tregarth, and led the way downstairs.

They had tea in a big old living room, overlooking the courtyard. Laura, still gathering impressions, was glad that the children talked so much. They were an attractive pair; in fact, Lelant was beautiful. A little, dark girl, with graceful movements. Elvan, now that she had a real chance to look at him, appealed to her more strongly than ever. He sat in a big chair near the window, wearing old grey trousers and an open-necked shirt, and, even so early in the year, his skin was tanned.

Rose was quiet and a little remote. She was making a valiant effort to hide her emotions, but she was lost in an incredulous dream because Peter Poldern was coming home.

"So you're going to take part in our May Day?" George Tregarth remarked, smiling across at Laura.

"Oh, yes. I'm looking forward to it so much. Rose said you'd tell me all about it," Laura said shyly.

"I'll tell you what I know, but there's a great deal that is lost in the mists of history. Even the song.... We don't know who Uncle Ben Trepol was. He's as mysterious as Aunt Ursula Birdwood in Padstow. Words get altered and corrupted as the centuries pass. Of course, when you just say the words they sound like doggerel. Most folk songs do. This is the first verse of the 'Day Song'," he said, and went on to recite:

"Sing, sing, for summer now is come,
   Green grow the leaves and white is the May-O;
   Dance one and all, follow the hoss,
   Rejoice on the morning of May-O!"

Isaac took up the words of the next verse:

"Oh, why is he dead? Oh, why did he die?
   Old Uncle Ben Trepol as well-O.
   The gulls they do cry, and fall from the sky,
   And loudly tolls the bell-O!"

"But I want to hear the tune!" Laura protested. "Rose says it brings people back across the world."

"It's unlucky to sing the song before May Day," Lelant said quickly.

"Luck!" said her father. "We're a superstitious lot in Cornwall. The Festival starts at midnight outside the Great Horse Inn. The 'hoss' is kept in a loft behind the Inn. Very like Padstow, where one of their two horses is kept behind the Golden Lion. Old Joseph will be heartbroken if he can't be here to take part. But Elvan says he thinks he'll be out of the hospital early next week. He has a mighty thick skull, it seems."

"But what exactly happened?" Rose asked, waking up from her absorbing thoughts.

"Someone bonked him out in the courtyard at two o'clock in the morning," Isaac explained, with faint relish.

"But who? Why? And why was he out of bed at that hour?"

"He says he heard a noise," George Tregarth explained. "Old sailors wake at the slightest sound, and of course you know his room is on the ground floor at the corner near the tower. He thinks someone fell on the uneven steps. So he got up and looked out and saw a light through one of the lancet windows."

"But there's nothing in the tower. Why would anyone—?"

"It's a complete mystery. Joe pulled on his trousers and put on his shoes and crept out the back door. He went over to the tower, but couldn't hear a sound or see anything, so he turned away and was walking beside the castle wall when someone attacked him from behind. That's all he knows. He didn't come round for an hour, and then he roused us all."

"But the police. . . . Didn't they find out who it was?"

"You know what the police are like here," said Rose's father. "Only three of them and pretty dumb, and there was nothing to help them, anyway. The only evidence was the fine bump on the back of Joe's head. A cut, too. They said at the hospital it was probably a large, fairly smooth stone, and there are plenty lying around."

"But didn't the dogs—?" Rose began.

"The dogs," said Mrs. Tregarth, "are getting old, and they've got into bad habits. Bill sleeps with Lellie, and Bob on Isaac's bed. I've argued until I'm tired, but there they are every night, and both rooms at the back of the house."

"You made them sleep in the shed the last few nights," Lelant said sadly, bending to fondle the ears of one old spaniel.

"And a lot of good it did. No one's likely to come again," George Tregarth said, lighting his pipe.

"I'm sure you girls would like to unpack now," said Mrs. Tregarth. "We have an invitation to dinner up at Poldern Place tonight. The Polderns thought Laura would like to see the house, and they've asked Arthur Pengwern, too."

"That will be nice, won't it, Laura?" Rose said, bending to pick up a cat.

Back in her room, seeing the early evening light

deepening over the grey roofs of Trepoldern and lying brilliantly over the North Cliff, where there was a solitary tower, Laura could hardly believe in reality. The fascination of the Tregarths . . . the mystery of old Joseph's attacker . . . the whole romantic Cornish scene and the prospect of dinner at the house on the opposite hill. And then, of course, to crown it all, there was May Day!

She put her things away, laid out her prettiest dress on the bed, and stood at the window dreaming. Except for the distant screaming of a gull, the whole place was wrapped in silence. The port below seemed to be asleep. Yet, in a few days' time, it would awaken to an ancient, compelling tune and to a "horse" dancing through the narrow streets. It was all very strange and quite the most interesting thing that had ever happened to her.

At seven o'clock Laura and Rose were ready to leave, Laura in her charming blue dress and Rose in a dark pink one that suited her perfectly. She seemed, since hearing the news of Peter Poldern's imminent return, to have taken on a new, dreamy glow. In London Laura had often thought her perhaps a little hard, but she looked quite different now. And yet she might well be in for more pain. Say Peter had fallen in love in Canada?

"Elvan's going to take you in his car, Laura," Mrs. Tregarth explained.

The two children, the spaniels and the cats hovered around a large Vauxhall. Apparently the shabby old car belonged to Elvan.

"They might have asked *us*," said Lelant wistfully.

"When you're older they will. This is a proper dinner party. You know you can go over to the Place whenever you like."

"But we'd enjoy a proper dinner party."

"Go and enjoy your scrambled eggs," her father said lightly. George Tregarth looked very different now, dressed for the evening. He was a handsome and rather intimidating man, and Laura was well on the way to worshipping him from afar. In fact, she was well on the way to worshipping the whole family. Her own home, while very pleasant, was conventional, and here she couldn't get over the feeling of being in a story.

Elvan, when he arrived in the courtyard, had also taken trouble with his appearance, but she decided she liked him better in the old fawn duffle coat in which she had first seen him.

"There's no need to be shy with the Polderns," Elvan said, as he followed the Vauxhall down the bumpy road. "You'll like them; they're very charming people. And it's a lovely old house, though they only live in a corner of it now. They own a lot of land still, and two farms, but it's poor land around here and they're anything but rich."

They drove through Trepoldern and took a narrow, climbing road. Soon they were up on higher ground and passed through open gates. Ahead lay the house, built of greystone and with mullioned windows. It was four centuries old, and looked as though it had grown out of the Cornish earth.

"There was an even older house," Elvan explained.

"The tower at the north end is all that was left of it after a fire."

They joined the others by the beautiful porch and were admitted by an old servant. He led them to a vast, very shabby drawing room, overlooking the river mouth and the shining evening sea. The Polderns were middleaged and quite ordinary, and it was really Arthur Pengwern who caught Laura's immediate attention. He was a heavily built, tough-looking young man, with a tanned skin; his manner was very friendly, perhaps, by English standards, over-friendly. His voice was loud and his Australian accent contrasted sharply with the soft, lilting tones of the others.

Laura and Rose asked for fruit drinks, but the others accepted sherry. Arthur singled Laura out and edged her toward one of the window embrasures.

"You're a stranger, too, aren't you? A Londoner? Oh, from Cheshire. That's in the North, isn't it? I've only been here a few days, so I still haven't got England very straight. Of course my father talked about it when I was a small kid, but I guess I've forgotten. I feel a terrible foreigner."

He must, having come so far. Laura sympathized, but wished she were with Elvan.

"But you belong here, in a kind of way. I gather your father grew up at the Vicarage," she said.

"Oh, yes, he was a loyal Trepoldern man. Every May Day he behaved as if he couldn't stand his exile another hour. I remember that. But he always said there were no prospects for him here."

"It was hard on his parents when he went away."

"It happens." The young man shrugged his big shoulders. "Of course they're dears, but very old and narrow-minded. I felt I had to see them and this place, but as to whether I'll stay. . . ."

"It is very quiet," said Laura.

"I come from Sydney, though I've been in the Outback, too. That was quiet, but Trepoldern is what you might call brooding. Can you understand this horse thing?"

"Not really," Laura admitted. "It's one of these strange survivals. There are others, I think. Hobby-horses at Padstow and Minehead, and morris dances . . . things like that. I'm looking forward to it."

"It may liven things up a bit."

The others were talking about Peter Poldern's return.

"Is he staying?" George Tregarth asked.

"We aren't sure," Mr. Poldern said, frowning. "We just had a cable saying he was flying to London tomorrow and hoped to arrive on Monday. But of course we hope he'll have shaken off that old restlessness. I could do with his help on the farms, and of course we've missed him terribly."

Dinner was announced then and they all went into a large, inadequately heated room. It was panelled in oak and very beautiful in its graceful shabbiness. Laura found herself seated between Mr. Poldern and Arthur, but Elvan was just opposite, so at least she could watch his face. She was a trifle bewildered by the pleasure it gave her.

The meal was simple; soup, roast beef and vegetables,

fruit salad and thick Cornish cream. But the table was elegantly laid and lighted by candles as the room grew darker, and the food was quietly served by the very old man servant. Laura tried to talk, but she increasingly felt that she was in a dream. Only that morning she had been in London.

Coffee was served in the drawing room and it was then that Mr. Poldern mentioned the mysterious attack on old Joseph.

"The police have no idea who it was?" he asked.

"As far as we know they haven't a notion, Mark," said George Tregarth. "Who *would* want to be in our tower at two o'clock in the morning? There's nothing there. Unless it was a tramp, wanting a bed for the night."

"Last year, for the Festival, we got some of those peculiar long-haired types, if you remember. Heaven knows what attracted them. I heard some arrived several days ago and are sleeping out. In fact, I caught a glimpse of one; a frightful creature with a guitar."

"Some more came today," said Rose. "We saw them."

"Yes, the police investigated them, but they seemed harmless. Rum types, as you say. Something about May Day does seem to appeal to them, and there'll be more by Thursday. The truth is that we're not used to trouble. The odd beating up by a drunken fisherman—"

"There was our mystery," said Mrs. Poldern, "but nothing really startling since then."

Her husband laughed, looking around the company.

"Our great mystery! And, of course, a tragedy, too, as old Charlie Zennor died."

Laura remembered that Rose had mentioned an old mystery and crime.

"What happened?" she asked. "Rose said there was something, but I didn't know it was anything to do with you."

4. The Poldern Mystery

"We're an old family," Mark Poldern said, as he poured himself some more coffee. "We've been here for untold ages. Our ancestors lived in Trepoldern Castle, then moved over here, and all we had left of those far off days were the Poldern cups. Medieval cups—gold, and decorated with jewels. Beyond price they were, in a way. Any museum in the world would have taken them, but we kept them here in this house. We thought of them as the Poldern Luck. And one night, twenty years ago, they were stolen."

"Really?" Laura was listening intently.

"They were kept in a glass case in this room. It was all fitted up with burglar alarms, of course. My father had kept them in a bank in Bodmin, but I thought it was absurd not to enjoy them. Such beautiful things. Some day," he added, "I might have let them go, but fate took a hand. Someone broke in, disconnected the alarm and got clean away with the cups. Charlie Zennor, who must have heard the intruder, was killed. We found his body in the morning. The cups have never been seen or heard of since."

"But surely they weren't readily saleable?" Arthur Pengwern remarked. "I mean, they wouldn't have been worth too much melted down, even though they were gold."

"That's true, of course. The only explanation was that they went to the kind of compulsive collector who just wanted to possess them, and didn't mind never being able to show them to people."

"But hadn't the police any ideas?" asked Laura.

"They had plenty of *ideas*. We had Scotland Yard down here; the local men couldn't handle it. They questioned every soul in the place and found out exactly nothing. No strangers had been known to be around. There was one local resident who came under some suspicion; Jack Penporth. He was a kind of odd-jobs man. He'd been a builder and also done some electrical work. He'd have known how to disconnect the wires and he was familiar with the house. I'd employed him from time to time, both here and at the farms. And he'd been in trouble before for petty theft. But the cups were far out of his class, and his wife swore he'd been in bed all that night."

"What happened to him?" asked Elvan.

"Oh, he and his wife and children went away to London eventually. I expect he came to a bad end, but I never heard." Mr. Poldern paused, then went on: "There's a kind of local legend that the cups are still here in Trepoldern, but we don't believe a word of it. Someone got away with them."

"You never used the insurance money," his wife pointed out.

"No-o. I did always hope they'd come back. Of course, we didn't get anything like their possible value. They were only insured for a few thousand."

"They're probably in some rich eccentric's collection," said George Tregarth. "Those were exciting days, weren't they? Normally we only wake up on May Day, but with all that Yard lot around it was different. I remember that Chief Inspector—what was his name? Brayne? No, Bright. He was determined to crack the case. We asked him to dinner, for the food was terrible at the Ship in those days. He must have been very cut up not to solve the affair."

"He's forgotten all about it now," said Mr. Poldern. "He must have had hundreds of cases since then. I suppose it just went down in the annals of Scotland Yard as an unsolved case. They must have plenty."

After that the talk became general, and thirty minutes later the guests rose to leave.

As they walked out into the hall, Arthur Pengwern said to Elvan:

"How about going fishing again tomorrow?"

"I'll see. Telephone you in the morning," Elvan answered, with slight reserve.

They all went out into the cold spring night. Trepoldern lay below, discernible only by a few widely spaced lights.

"Would you like a lift down into the town?" Elvan asked Arthur.

"Well, thanks. I'd better get back quickly. The old people settle down so early. I feel quite a rake being out this late." He climbed into the back of the car, talking all the time. "Interesting hearing about those old cups, wasn't it? I think I dimly remember my father talking about the theft when I was a kid. Of course he'd left by that time, but news travels and he kept in touch with the old folk until he died. Quite a lark if the cups turned up, after all!"

"They won't," said Elvan, driving carefully out of the gates and down the narrow, dark road.

"Oh, things happen. That's what you people here forget. So set in your ways."

Already they were in the little town. There were lights in the tiny square, but not a soul in sight. All the small houses and shops were in darkness. Elvan turned up a very narrow street called Church Lane.

"Oh, no need!" said Arthur Pengwern, with a loud laugh. "I still have the use of my legs."

"It's no trouble," Elvan said. He stopped the car in front of a Georgian house that was in utter darkness. Dimly Laura could see a church tower against the stars.

"Ten o'clock and the world asleep," said Arthur, climbing out. "I think I'll soon head for London and a bit of life."

"Well, it might be the best thing," Elvan remarked. "The old people will be sad, but if you're expecting excitement in Trepoldern you won't get it. Good night."

He turned the car in the churchyard gateway. When

they had passed the square and were climbing the road to the castle, Laura ventured:

"Do you like Arthur?"

"No, not much, but the Vicar asked me as a special favor to make him welcome and to do what I could. He won't stay. Only a saint would. They're a difficult old pair at the Vicarage, though Arthur persists in calling them dears. The house is dreary and the food awful. We all feel a responsibility for them, though."

He took the last part of the hill very fast and they swept into the courtyard. As Laura stood in the cold starlight she thought that none of it seemed real. Elvan seemed to realize some of her thoughts.

"You must find it a great change from London. I'm glad Rose is back."

The others seemed to have gone to their rooms and Laura went to hers, trying to sort out her endless impressions. Rose, already in her dressing gown, met her in the passage as she went to the bathroom.

"Sleep well, Laura!" she said.

"And you!" But would Rose sleep, when she looked so keyed up?

It was a long time before Laura herself drifted off into slumber. There was so much to think about; so many new experiences. She tried to put off thinking about Elvan, but after a restless hour she had to face the fact that she seemed on the edge of falling in love. After a few hours she felt more for Elvan than she had ever felt for Geoffrey or any other young man.

And it was silly. It was downright absurd and rather

shameful. She was just being the same as all the other girls Rose had mentioned, and hadn't she said Elvan was practically engaged? He had been nice, but then, of course, she was a guest in the house and he had to be polite.

She must try to forget Elvan.

During breakfast the next morning the telephone rang. George Tregarth went to answer it and came back to say:

"That was Mark Poldern. They had a little trouble in the night up at the Place."

"Trouble?" Everyone was immediately alert.

"Yes. He doesn't sleep too well and sometimes gets up to fix himself a snack at three or four o'clock. He happened to look out of his bedroom window and saw a light in the old tower that adjoins the house. He hurried as much as he could, but slipped on the stairs in his haste and slightly twisted his ankle. By the time he got outside, the tower was dark and there wasn't a sound anywhere."

There was a silence around the breakfast, then Lelant cried, wide-eyed:

"Their tower as well as ours!"

"Yes, that's mysterious, isn't it?" Isaac agreed.

"You read too many mysteries," their father said, a trifle sharply. "It must be a coincidence."

"But who *would* be in the Poldern Place tower?" Mrs. Tregarth asked, frowning. "There's nothing there, as far as I know."

Two towers! Laura glanced out the window, but, from the room they were in, saw only the castle walls. It flashed through her mind that there were at least two other towers in Trepoldern; the lonely one on the North Cliff, and, of course, the church tower. But she told herself that it couldn't mean anything.

5. Laura Asks Questions

"What are you and Laura going to do this morning?" Mrs. Tregarth asked Rose after a while.

"I'll take her for a walk along the path toward the sea," said Rose, waking from a dream. She had not managed to sleep well and her eyes looked tired, facts that her mother noticed without comment.

"Good! Some more toast, Laura?" Mrs. Tregarth asked briskly. If there was a mystery in Trepoldern it was instantly dispelled by her tone and by the bright, cool April morning.

George Tregarth had just risen from the table when the front door bell rang. They heard Bess go to open the door, there was the sound of voices, then she appeared in the dining room.

"Please, Mr. Tregarth, a gentleman wants to see you. Elderly and a bit odd-looking, you might say." Bess had been with the family for many years and usually said what she thought.

"What does he want? I was just leaving for the farm. It's early for callers," George Tregarth said resignedly.

"He didn't say. But his name is Summer."

"Not Winter or Spring?" said Isaac, and he and Lelant began to giggle. Their mother glanced at them reprovingly, for the dining room door was open.

At that moment a figure appeared in the doorway. Laura instantly recognized the ancient raincoat and the wild hair.

"It's the folklorist," she murmured. "He was on the train."

With fussy apology, Mr. Summer surged into the room.

"You must pardon me for intruding, but I was anxious. . . . Dear me! You're still at breakfast! My dear sir, have I the pleasure of addressing Mr. George Tregarth? My name is Solomon Summer. My apologies to you and all these charming ladies." His glance included Lelant, who collapsed into uncontrollable giggles. Her mother put her hand on her shoulder and whisked her out of the room.

George Tregarth was not a man to suffer fools gladly, though natural courtesy warred with his more impatient side.

"Good morning, Mr. Summer," he said briskly. "What can I do for you?"

Mr. Summer's eyes roved over the table.

"But I have interrupted your breakfast! I'm an early bird myself, and at the inn they told me that you managed a farm. I had thought, even on Sunday, I might have missed you."

"I don't manage it, I own it," said George Tregarth.

"But I only give part of my time to farming. As it happens, I was just leaving."

"Then perhaps I might make an appointment for another occasion? You see, I wish to presume on your great knowledge of old customs. I've read your books and greatly admired them. I am a folklorist and I have always promised myself a visit to Trepoldern on May Day. Now, at last, here I am. So strange a thing, the Festival of the Great Horse. Well, of course I realize that there are others here and there. Padstow, of course. . . . I should greatly enjoy," he ended, perhaps sensing George Tregarth's impatience, "a talk with you."

"Well, why don't you come up for a drink tonight after dinner?" George Tregarth asked resignedly. "Say, nine o'clock."

"May I? That will be delightful. I shall so enjoy it. Meanwhile, I'll acquaint myself with your quiet little town and its charming people. So very extraordinary how these things linger in remote corners. But I won't keep you now." He gave a kind of bow in the direction of Laura and Rose, ignored Isaac, who was snuffling into his handkerchief, and turned to the door with a toss of his wild head.

When he had gone, it was Rose who started to giggle.

"He had a look of the hoss!" she gasped. "The way he moved as he went. I could almost see. . . . Oh, Father, you're in for it tonight!"

"I'm afraid so," agreed George Tregarth. But he looked rather sternly at his small son, who had emerged from his handkerchief to reveal watering eyes. "Really,

Isaac! You and Lellie are revolting sometimes."

"But a saint would have wanted to laugh," Isaac protested.

"Well, a saint wouldn't, all the same. Of course he must be some kind of gentle nut. We do get them for May Day. I must be off. Have a good time, girls." And he strode away.

Elvan had been a silent, inscrutable watcher of the proceedings. Now he laughed.

"Quite like a play! I thought he looked odd yesterday, but he's worse than I thought."

"Are you coming walking with us?" Rose asked.

"No-o. I think I'd better telephone Arthur and go fishing for a few hours. I have him on my conscience, little as I like it."

Laura had started the morning with several good resolutions, but she was conscious of a feeling of letdown. She told herself firmly not to be silly. She would be there for two weeks and would have plenty of time to get to know Elvan. But, if possible, she wasn't going to think about him at all.

She and Rose set off on their walk soon after ten o'clock. Outside the sheltering castle walls the wind was cold, though the air sparkled with sunlight. But it was warmer down in the town. Trepoldern seemed more deeply asleep than it had done on the previous afternoon. It dreamed in sunny silence; the little shops were closed, and in the square a few old men sat on a bench. It seemed very far from the world, and that was presumably how the Festival of the Great Horse had

Laura Asks Questions   53

survived the passing of countless centuries.

"All the same," said Laura, speaking her thoughts aloud, "I can't imagine May Day. People singing and dancing, following the horse!"

Rose, who had been in a remote mood, thinking about Peter's return the next day, laughed.

"Oh, May Day is different, my dear. Everyone is out to have a good time. The fattest old women and the baldest old men will be in the streets, singing and teasing the horse."

"Teasing it? How?"

"Oh, there's always a teaser. People take turns. They dance in front of the horse, and they wave a piece of painted wood fastened to a stick. It's a kind of baton; green, black and white. We call ours the Green Horse sometimes. In Padstow they have two, the red hoss and the blue. I'll show you where our hoss is kept."

They turned up a narrow ancient street, where the fronts of the cottages leaned forward over the cobblestones. At the top was a very small, very old inn, and over the door was a crude painting of the hobby-horse; a grotesque creature, circular and black, with a tiny head and tail, and, in the very center of the great round body, a second head ending in a point.

"That pointed thing is the mask," Rose explained. "It goes over the head of the man inside the framework, covering his face and hiding his identity. Father will tell you that the point indicates they originally worshipped a unicorn, not a horse at all. It was a supernatural being, of course; an old god. The framework and mask are kept in the loft behind."

"Brooding there, waiting for May Day," murmured Laura. She would have liked to ask a great many questions, but Rose had turned away and was walking rapidly along another narrow street that led to the harbor. The subject seemed to be closed.

The tide was high, a few boats lay at anchor, and sea gulls screamed over the river. There were a few more old men, but Laura's attention was at once caught by the noisy group of young men, who were with two or three equally scruffy and bizarre-looking girls. They really were a strange crowd to see in a remote Cornish fishing port. All the men had very long hair and were dressed in bright colors, and one, a big young man with a beard, was strumming a guitar.

Rose looked at them with distaste.

"I wish the police could send them away, but they said last year that if they did they might come back in force and wreck the place. It's happened in other seaside towns in England, but more with the motorcycle gangs, the leather-jacket lot. This kind are more peaceful, and I suppose they don't actually do any harm."

They were past the group by then and turning up a path that climbed to the North Cliff.

"The one with the beard is the worst!" said Laura laughing. "You can hardly see him for all that hair. I wonder when he last had a bath? They'd certainly be more at home in London."

As they climbed between the sweet-smelling stretches of grass and gorse bushes, they saw that there were a few rough tents pitched in sheltered places. Outside one of them a young man in an orange shirt and tan trousers was plucking at a banjo. He stared at them, but offered no greeting. A few mocking twangs followed them up the path.

Rose had fallen silent again and her face had a lost, enchanted look. Laura felt shut out, but sympathized deeply. She stopped and stared back at the castle walls on the opposite cliff. The tower stood up strongly, and she could see the roof of the Tregarths' house.

The tower reminded her of Joseph's mysterious attacker, and she swiveled around until she could just glimpse Poldern Place, high on the hill to their left. There, too, a less ruined tower stood up equally strongly. And in that tower, too, there had seemed to be an intruder. There must surely be some connection.

Immediately above them, at the top of the cliff path, was the third tower, apparently whole.

"Why should anyone be interested in towers?" she asked. Rose jumped and stared at her.

"What?"

"Someone in your tower, and last night someone in the one at Poldern Place. Can you think of any reason why someone should be interested in them?"

"Oh, I don't suppose there was any connection," Rose answered vaguely. "Unless it was some of those awful newcomers looking for a place to sleep."

"Well, I suppose they might. Can anyone get into the

Poldern Place tower? Is it ever locked?"

"It never used to be locked. It isn't actually reached from the house and there's nothing there. Peter and I always played there when we were children. He's older, but we were always great friends," she ended sadly.

"So you'd know if there was anything—well, unusual?"

"There's nothing," Rose assured her. "Peter used to keep his biggest toys in the little groundfloor room. They did keep the door to the battlements locked, because the coping wasn't safe. But it was probably repaired years ago."

"All the same—" Laura's mind was still playing on the slight mystery. "Why was this tower we're coming to built?"

"Oh, it's just a lookout. Napoleonic Wars, or something of the kind. Not really old like the others."

"I wonder if there have been lights here, too?"

Rose looked at Laura with some amusement.

"You're as bad as the children. Fond of mysteries and thrillers. There's no real mystery."

Her slightly superior tone nettled and silenced Laura. Probably it was one of the long-haired types who had attacked Joseph. But why should anyone have done anything so drastic? The old man would probably have done no worse than order him off the Tregarths' property, and, in any case, he had seen no one. But could the intruder have been sure of that?

Oh, well, she told herself, Rose might be right and

she was being childish and silly. And the view, as they topped the rise and saw the gorse-covered cliff walk all the way to the river mouth and the sea, was enough to take her breath away.

6. The Third Tower

They passed the lookout tower without stopping, but as Rose went first over a stone stile, Laura glanced back at it. There was an open door on the landward side, but the place seemed deserted. There was certainly no one up on what must be a flat roof.

They walked slowly the delightful two miles to where the River Poldern opened out into the sea. Here there was a deep cove, with shining black rocks against which the rising tide washed gently for a day in spring. Laura could imagine what it must be like in wild weather.

At that point a rough road ended not far from the cliff edge and a couple of cars were parked, their occupants down in the cove.

"In summer it gets pretty crowded," said Rose, as they went cautiously down the cliff path. Laura began to pick up unusual shells and her wandering took her toward the gaping black mouth of a cave.

"The Cave of the Great Horse, local people call it," Rose explained, as they peered into the sea-smelling gloom. "There's a legend that the Trepoldern horse came from here. Father says it was probably used for some kind of rites in ancient times. We'd better go, though. The tide's rising fast. It fills the cave this time of year."

On the way back, fairly close inshore they saw a boat in which two young men were fishing. One wore a familiar blue sweater. Laura had seen Elvan in it at breakfast time.

Rose waved and shouted and the young men waved back.

"Elvan must have taken sandwiches," said Rose. "Otherwise he'll be late for lunch."

Elvan did not return for lunch and Laura was again conscious of disappointment. Mrs. Tregarth told Rose that some old family friends were coming over from Bodmin that afternoon. They were very eager to see Rose again.

"Don't worry if you want to go exploring," she said kindly to Laura. "Tea will be about four-thirty. The weather may not stay like this for long, so make the best of it."

"If you won't think me rude—"

"Just do as you like here," said George Tregarth. "We're easy, so long as you're not lonely. Ask the children to go with you."

But by then Isaac had left the table and disappeared, and Laura saw Lelant walking slowly across the courtyard with a book under her arm. She went through the broken doorway of the tower as Laura started in pursuit. The little girl fascinated her, for she had never had a sister. Besides, she wanted to see the tower.

There was nothing much to see, however. A broken stone stair spiralled its way upward, with an occasional lancet window to let in light. Apart from a couple of embrasures and a totally empty stone room halfway up, there was nothing but the prospect of a view from the top. The tower had probably been built as a lookout in a century long before the Napoleonic Wars. Laura realized she didn't know which invaders might have come in those remote ages.

At the top of the stairs an opening without a door gave access to the roof, and there was Lelant. She was sitting comfortably with her back against the ramparts, in a sunny corner sheltered from the sea wind. She looked startled for a moment, then smiled.

"Hullo! I often read here in summer, and it's lovely today. When I was young it was my secret fortress. Bess couldn't reach me here. She has rheumatism and hates the steps."

When she was young! But Laura didn't laugh. She wanted to make friends with Lelant and Isaac.

"It's a beautiful place," she said, looking over the battlements to the silent town below. "Won't you sing the May Day song for me?"

Lelant squinted up at her against the sun.

"It really would be unlucky. Maybe the hoss would chase me. It frightens me when he does . . . so huge and black and tossing. Of course, he doesn't usually chase us. Last year he chased two strangers almost into the harbor!"

"But are you really afraid of the horse? I don't understand at all. It's only a man in a kind of covering."

"It's a black tarpaulin on a great heavy frame," Lelant said gravely. "I met the hoss when I was a baby. I've been right under the frame, dancing, too. You can get under when you're small. But there is something a bit frightening, though everyone's so gay all day. It's so old, you see. Father says it generates some feeling. You *know* it's just a man; sometimes Billy Bailey from the Great Horse Inn. The men take turns, as it's such hard work dancing with that great thing on their shoulders. But when you can't see them, not always even their feet. . . . Well, you'll see on May Day. Father plays a drum."

More and more strange. George Tregarth playing a drum at the Festival of the Great Horse! Laura would have liked to hear more, but Lelant was fingering her book, politely trying to hide the fact that she wanted to read.

As Laura went carefully down the stairs she heard Isaac calling from below: "Lellie! Where are you?"

He passed Laura carefully on a narrow part of the stairs and went rapidly upwards.

"I want to talk to you, Lellie. It's important!" she heard him say loudly. The acoustics of the tower brought the words to Laura clearly, though she was by then almost at the bottom.

She saw the visitors arriving in a big blue car as she started down the narrow road to the town. Alone she could really savor the atmosphere of Trepoldern and she wandered for some time through the narrow streets. Lelant's talk had given her a growing sense of something pending. In that loft behind the inn the horse waited—yet it was nonsense to feel that it had a life of its own.

Presently she found herself climbing the path up to the North Cliff again. The tents were all deserted; the campers were all down by the harbor, annoying the conservative old men by their presence.

The lookout tower loomed ahead, square and rather grim. She was curious about it, but she sat under a gorse bush for several minutes, searching the river for Elvan and Arthur in their boat. When there was no sign of them she rose and walked the last few yards over open land to the door, which was half off its hinges and clearly would not close.

The steps ahead were very dark, but seemed in better repair than the ones at the castle. She began to climb slowly and rather hesitantly, but she was determined to see if there could be anything of interest in the third tower.

There were not many windows to let in the light, and suddenly it seemed eerie. When she heard a sound above her she stiffened and her heart beat more quickly. Yet it was probably only a holiday maker who had been up to see the view.

There were definitely feet coming down, rather heavily. Laura's groping hand displaced a small loose stone in the wall and it fell with a sharp rattle. The footsteps above stopped abruptly, as though someone were listening. She remembered that she had seen no one on top of the tower as she approached, but the last few yards over the grassland had taken only seconds and he could have left the top before she emerged from under the gorse bush.

The footsteps were coming on again. In a ridiculous panic, Laura almost turned and rushed down the steps, but she stopped herself in time. A sprained ankle would ruin her holiday.

So she stood pressed against the wall, waiting to see who might appear above her.

She saw first a pair of shabby, heavy shoes, then frayed trouser legs. As the man eased himself around a tricky corner on the narrow stair Laura saw with relief that it was only the harmless lunatic, Mr. Solomon Summer, folklorist.

Mr. Summer, in his turn, seemed relieved to see Laura. He stopped, ran a hand through his abundant grey hair, and smiled at her, as she stood there in the faint light from an opening below.

"Good afternoon, my dear. A somewhat unusual place to meet! These stairs are too steep and narrow for my liking, but I was anxious to see the view. So interesting, these old towers. When I heard you I was afraid I was going to meet a horde of holiday makers. So difficult to pass, in that case."

"You'd have seen them coming up the path," said Laura, still leaning against the wall.

"I'm somewhat shortsighted. It goes with my advancing years, I'm afraid. One is resigned to suffering from something, and I find glasses such a nuisance. I'm always losing them." He paused and then added: "If you want to go to the top I'll be delighted to escort you, Miss —Tregarth, is it?"

"I'm Laura Edmund, from London. I'm only staying with the Tregarths. Oh, please don't bother to come up again." He looked so old and vague that Laura was afraid he might collapse or something, and she certainly didn't want his company. But he had turned and was leading the way fleetly enough.

"It's a trifle tricky getting from the last step on to the roof. I am always willing to help attractive ladies."

"Old idiot!" thought Laura. But, all the same, it was pleasant to be called an attractive lady, especially when she was wearing old green slacks and a bulky sweater, with her hair untidy from the sea wind.

Mr. Summer was talking as he climbed. His voice echoed back from the stone walls that enclosed them.

"Dear me! I had such a disappointing morning. The people of Trepoldern are certainly a close-mouthed lot. I hoped that some of the older people would talk into my tape recorder, telling me their memories of past May Days and just what the affair means to them. But they were really quite rude. . . . I felt rebuffed."

"Rose Tregarth says they don't really like strangers to come and take an interest. They're quite upset by all the peculiar types that are here already." Laura stopped abruptly, because he was undoubtedly a peculiar type himself and she had been tactless. But Mr. Summer, turning to help her on to the roof, seemed unaware of any possible connection with himself.

"Yes, I gathered that, too. One woman said she'd have them run out of the town, but the police won't. But such very strange clothes, I do agree. I find myself wanting to understand their interest in the Festival. I shall try to talk to them."

"I'd sooner keep away from them," said Laura. "Did you see the big young man with a guitar? I thought he looked awful. So tough and hairy." Then once more she realized her lack of tact. Really, her silly tongue! Mr. Summer himself had a great deal of hair.

To cover up her remark, she walked around the tower, commenting on the view, which was very fine on that clear spring day. Blue river and sea . . . short green grass . . . the blaze of yellow gorse.

There were two or three stone benches below the parapet, and Mr. Summer sat down, motioning to Laura to sit beside him. She hesitated, only wanting to leave him, and not quite knowing how to get away.

"I really must go now," she began. "I promised to be back for tea, and I want to see the last tower."

"The *last* tower?"

"Oh, I meant the church tower." Laura cursed her tongue again.

"You're interested in church architecture, or merely in towers in general?" He was looking at her in surprise.

"No. *Yes.*" Rose had thought her mad, but in a way Mr. Summer had a courtly and sympathetic air. And it couldn't have been Mr. Summer in the castle tower several nights ago, because he had only arrived on the train yesterday. Well, of course it hadn't been Mr. Summer! Why would an elderly folklorist clamber about in a private place in the middle of the night?

"I had a silly idea," Laura told him quickly. "My friend laughed at me, but I still thought I'd take a closer look. You see, the old servant, Joseph, up at Trepoldern Castle saw a light in their tower—" She told him briefly what had happened, then went on to describe Mr. Poldern's experience of the previous night. "Well, it did seem funny. . . . lights in two of the towers. Only I can think of no reason why. But there are four towers in all, so I just thought I'd look and see if anything could possibly interest anyone."

"Such as what?" Mr. Summer was scratching the stone bench with a spent match. She didn't know if he were interested or not.

"That's the trouble; I haven't the least idea. What could it be? Oh, it was probably just some of the strangers, looking for a place to sleep. Some of them have tents, but last year, I was told, some of them slept in the bus shelter. Yet surely this would be the tower they'd choose. The other two are on private land, so close to houses."

Laura smiled and nodded and went toward the door that led to the steps. Mr. Summer rose and followed her.

"Please permit me to go first. Going down a spiral staircase is always worse than coming up."

Laura began to wish she had snubbed him in the first place. She must be ten times more nimble than her companion, and she certainly needed no help. But he was going first anyway, courteously stepping past her. He almost bowed, and Laura almost giggled in his face.

She followed him down the tower, making up her mind to say a quick goodbye as soon as they reached the bottom. She deeply regretted her friendlier impulses.

7. Another Intruder

But Laura's plans came to nothing, for Mr. Summer stayed at her side, walking quite briskly. A little way down the path they met Lelant and Isaac, coming up. Remembering the giggles at the breakfast table, Laura tried to hurry her companion past the two children, but he paused to greet them.

"How lucky you are to live in this beautiful place! I expect you're looking forward to May Day?"

"Oh, yes. We don't have to go to school," Lelant said, quite politely.

Catching Isaac's eye, Laura really didn't trust the conversation to go far. So she nodded and hurried off down the path, and at once Mr. Summer followed, regaining her side in a few seconds. As they continued on their way down into the town he asked a lot of questions about the Tregarths and said how much he was looking forward to his talk with George Tregarth that evening.

"The church, I think, is fifteenth century," he offered, still with Laura as she turned decisively up Church Lane. "I heard that the Vicar is growing old and rather feeble, but I hope I can persuade him to talk to me about his feelings concerning the Festival. It's Sunday, of course. A busy day for Vicars. Maybe I'll call on him tomorrow morning. A service at this hour, do you think? Sunday School, perhaps. It's just after three-thirty." But the church, when they pushed open the heavy, creaking door, seemed empty and very cold, with a musty smell.

"Oh, I don't think I'll bother," said Laura, repelled by the silence and the ancient odor. "Probably the tower door's locked, anyway."

"You're giving up your little mystery?" Mr. Summer asked, looking disappointed. "You don't think anyone is interested in the four towers, after all?"

"No. It was just a silly notion. Too much imagination."

"But here's the door, and it isn't locked. We would get a bird's eye view of the town."

Laura drew back from the dark opening. Suddenly and inexplicably she didn't care for Mr. Summer's company at all. There was something too eager about him, and the church seemed lonely, even eerie.

"No, I—There really isn't time now."

"Well, then, I will say good-bye for the time being. Tonight we'll meet again, I hope. I'll just take a look at the tower, since I'm here, and then maybe I'll tackle the long pull up to Poldern Place. Mr. Mark Poldern may perhaps have some anecdotes about the horse—"

Clearly he meant to bother everyone in his pursuit of knowledge. Laura was just turning away when a noise

70   The May Day Mystery

up the dark tower made her jump violently. Mr. Summer also looked startled.

Footsteps descended the last few stairs and Arthur Pengwern appeared. He looked so very ordinary that Laura laughed. Really she must be growing nervous after hearing the stories about lights in the towers. Arthur looked very suntanned, even in the dim light, and he had a camera slung over his shoulder.

"Oh, hullo!" he said to Laura, and her first impression that his rather heavy face was frowning was quickly dispelled.

"I thought you were out fishing with Elvan," Laura remarked.

"Came back an hour ago. Are you going up the tower?" He was staring in puzzled surprise at Mr. Summer. "I've just been taking pictures of the Vicarage from the top. Quite an interesting angle."

"No. I'm not going up now. This is Mr. Solomon Summer. He's a folklorist. Arthur Pengwern is the Vicar's grandson, just back from Australia," she told Mr. Summer.

"A wonderful country, I should think," said Mr. Summer. "I have never had the pleasure of going there. You were there on a visit?"

"I was born in Sydney. My father emigrated. My parents died when I was ten and I was adopted by my mother's mother. Now she's dead and I remembered hearing stories of Trepoldern from my father, so I thought I'd come and get to know the old people,"

Arthur explained. Laura was faintly surprised that he went into such detail for a stranger.

"Your father must have found Sydney a change from a Cornish fishing village. He was young when he went?" Mr. Summer sounded only politely interested.

"Not very. About twenty-five," said Arthur shortly, obviously wishing he had not launched into the conversation. "That was twenty-four years ago. He married an Australian girl soon after he arrived." Then he turned firmly to Laura. "May I walk somewhere with you?"

"I'm going back to the castle," said Laura.

"Then I'll walk some of the way with you. Things are pretty slack," Arthur confessed gloomily, as they left the church. "If I'm staying I'll have to get a job. Fishing and photography are pleasant enough, but they don't make money, and the old people don't have much, that's clear."

"What is your job?" Laura asked curiously. He didn't look like an intellectual type.

"I haven't really got one," Arthur said frankly. "I mean, not what you'd call a profession. My father was an educated man. Well, naturally, I guess, being a clergyman's son. But my mother's family were simple folk and I don't seem to have inherited many brains. I went off to the Outback when I was eighteen. Worked on a sheep farm. Drove a truck. All this is a bit of a shock. A Georgian Vicarage and my grandparents."

"I gather they're a bit tiresome," Laura remarked.

"Well, yes. I hate to say it, but they are." His tone was frank and rueful. "Granny's an invalid. . . . Well, I expect you'll meet them. She likes to know what's going on, and as you're a friend of the Tregarths, you're going to be asked to a meal. I hope you'll come. I could do with a pretty girl around."

Laura didn't answer. She didn't want to be his pretty girl. She stole a look at his face, contrasting him with Elvan. Arthur certainly had Cornish cheekbones and he was dark, too, but he was taller than Elvan, and at the same time, more thick-set. The difference was, however, mainly in the expression. Arthur was probably rather stupid, and Elvan, she had no doubt, had brains and imagination. Those eyebrows, and his eyes and hands. She could still see his hands on the wheel. But really she mustn't dwell on Elvan. To fall in love so quickly was folly. She would only go away and suffer like Rose. But how did you stop a thing that seemed already started?

"I've bought an old car," said Arthur. "I'm taking possession of it in the morning. I hope it goes—it cost next to nothing. And that leaves me almost at the end of my cash."

"I suppose you'll have to get a job then," said Laura.

They had left the town and were climbing the narrow road to the castle. And there, sitting on an earthen bank as they rounded a corner, was Elvan. He nodded to Arthur and smiled at Laura.

"I was sent to look for you and saw you coming. Tea's ready early and the visitors will be leaving soon after.

"Then I'll say good-bye for now," said Arthur. "I'm expected for tea at the Vicarage. Been out all day. . .

frowned on on a Sunday. Missed morning church, but not my line."

"He'll never fit into that household," Elvan remarked, as they approached the castle walls. "What do you think of Trepoldern?"

"I love it! I can't believe I only left London yesterday."

Tea was ready in the living room. The children came in with the dogs a few minutes later and the big room seemed quite crowded. The visitors were a middleaged couple named Sennan, and Mrs. Sennan talked a good deal. Laura sat near the window, her eyes ranging from face to face. George Tregarth looked bored and Rose was rather feverishly animated. Lelant and Isaac ate a good deal, and talked and giggled with their heads close together. Their mother reprimanded them once or twice and they quieted down.

"I hope you aren't going to find it dull, Laura," Mrs. Tregarth said, when she returned from seeing off the visitors. "We lead a quiet life."

Laura denied it fiercely. Dull? When Trepoldern had already laid a strange spell on her. When there was Elvan and so many interesting things for her mind to play on. Lights in towers. . . Mr. Summer and his odd behavior. . . Peter Poldern coming home so romantically to the old house on the opposite hill. The story of the lost Poldern cups also fascinated her, even though there was never likely to be an explanation of their whereabouts.

She couldn't say all that to Mrs. Tregarth, though.

"I love the country and being in Cornwall. I'm so happy!"

She was happier still an hour later when Elvan suggested that she and Rose might like to have dinner in Polperro or Looe.

"It's not so far," he said. "And Laura should see the South Coast."

Rose said she'd stay at home with her mother, as they still had a lot to talk about.

"But you and Laura go. It's a lovely evening."

Laura, ordered to put on something warm as the wind would be cold when the sun went down, rushed away to get ready. A drive with Elvan, and dinner in one of those interesting old fishing villages! She stared at her flushed face in the glass and felt her cheeks tingling. Not only with the sun and sea wind, but also with excitement. But she was also a little scared. It was nice of Elvan to entertain the guest, but what if her conversation bored him? He was four or five years older, and what about all the other girls he knew? What about the girl to whom he might be almost engaged? The thought stabbed sharply into her happiness.

But Elvan didn't seem to expect to be bored. He raised a tuneful voice in song as he drove the big, old car rather fast along the road to Bodmin. Laura laughed and relaxed, watching his hands on the wheel and stealing glances at his profile.

"Perhaps *you'll* sing me the May Song," she ventured, as they weaved their way through Bodmin and headed out into the country again.

"Do I hear a ring of challenge in your voice?" he asked, looking amused.

"No. No, of course not. But I asked Lelant and she wouldn't. She insisted that it was unlucky."

"Superstitious child!" Elvan said placidly.

"Then—"

"You'll hear it hundreds of times on May Day."

Laura didn't press the matter, but her feeling of curiosity and anticipation grew. In the heart of Trepoldern clearly lay a very strange and ancient thing, and even Elvan, who, she had learned from Rose, had been at London University and now had some kind of scientific job at a new factory near Redruth, was Cornishman enough to respect the old beliefs. A scientist! Well, it was very odd indeed.

They had dinner at a hotel in Polperro, then walked the narrow streets in the dusk. Elvan talked about Cornwall and about his family; he told her a little about his job.

"Sometimes," he said, "I think I'll give it all up and help Father with the farm. It's a more real life."

It was lovely to be driven through the spring night and Laura just relaxed and listened. This was something that might never happen to her again.

"Do you drive?" Elvan asked, toward the end of the trip.

"Yes. My father taught me and I passed my test. But of course I don't get a chance in London."

"You can drive this car one day, if you like," said Elvan.

"Would you really let me?" Oh, perhaps she would have more of his company!

"Of course." They had been climbing the hill to the castle and Elvan suddenly stopped the car just short of the walls. "Let's get out and look at the view."

There was a young moon faintly lighting the roofs of Trepoldern. The air was cold and smelled of the sea, and the harbor, faintly shining, lay asleep. But on the North Cliff there were dim lights, the glow of a fire, and the twanging of a guitar—the sound came to them clearly on the night air. Someone, perhaps the hairy young tough, though she had seen others with musical instruments, was playing "Waltzing Matilda."

The night was so beautiful, and Elvan so close, that Laura was happier than she had ever been in her life. It had been an enchanted evening; a long and lovely day. Tomorrow she would be sensible, but just now she could only savor the last moments.

When they reached the house Mr. Summer had gone and George Tregarth was writing in his study with the door open.

"That man's a fool or lunatic!" he said, turning to them as they passed. "And he's been up at Poldern Place, too. I told him as much as I thought good for him, really almost as much as I know. There are so few records. I only hope he doesn't give a talk about the hoss on radio. I thought I knew his voice, and he admitted he had given a few talks."

Laura spoke to Rose briefly and then went to bed, but couldn't sleep. At one o'clock she was tired of tossing and turning and got out of bed without switching on the light. The small moon was still bright and there was enough light for her to see a dark figure just leaving the tower. The figure was no more than a shadow, immediately swallowed up in the darker shadows under the castle walls.

8. *Laura Listens*

Laura stiffened and watched intently, and in another few seconds the figure showed again briefly in the wide opening where the gateway had once been. Her window was open, but no sound reached her from the stony road. The intruder must have been wearing rubber-soled shoes.

The April air was very cold and she shivered, wondering if there was anything she should do. Rouse the house? Slip on a few clothes and go after the man? Well, she had thought it was a man. Hard to be sure, but something about the way the dim figure had moved—

Common sense told her that neither course would yield results. The visitor had gone, must be halfway down to the town by now, the sleeping town that seemed to hide secrets.

She went back to bed and eventually slept. In the morning it seemed like a dream, for the sun was shining again, the view was dazzling and a few fishing boats showed some activity. She could see tiny figures moving about on their decks.

Rose came in, flushed and very attractive in her red sweater and dark grey slacks.

"Oh, Laura, he'll be here this afternoon! I couldn't sleep at first, thinking of him actually in London last night. I wonder how soon I'll see him?"

"Oh, Rose, it is wonderful for you, but—"

"Yes, I'm a fool. He didn't care when he went away, and why should he care now? But at the moment all that matters is just seeing him, hearing his voice. I've been so starved all these months. . . I suppose you don't understand?"

Two days ago it might have been true, but Laura was learning something new and painful. She had thought herself in love, really in love, once before, when she was sixteen, but to her surprise the feeling had died quite quickly. This new feeling wouldn't go so easily, she was certain. Elvan was no callow boy.

"I hope you'll be very happy," she said soberly.

When they went down the rest of the family were already gathered around the table. Breakfast was early, because the children had to go to school. Laura accepted bacon and eggs from Bess and then told them what she had seen in the night. Lelant and Isaac gasped and then turned to stare at each other, Mrs. Tregarth looked worried, and George Tregarth indignant.

"It's too bad!" he exclaimed. "Those hippies or whatever they are again, I suppose. Well, I'll ring the police, but they're less than no good. Where were the dogs?"

The children looked guilty and Elvan laughed.

"They're too old to be any use," he said. "And there's no evidence against the strangers."

"No, but who else would have attacked old Joseph? I'm sure that lot are all no-good types."

Elvan now looked amused by his father.

"That's a middleaged point of view, Dad. Some of them do look ghastly, but others may have taken their vacations here because they feel a genuine interest in the Festival. No money for hotels."

"You may be right, but I doubt it. I never saw a more raffish crowd in my life. Mark Poldern says he's going to lock the gates of the Place at night, but he knows that won't keep out anyone determined to get in. The walls are falling down in a dozen places. And they haven't even a dog nearer than the farm. Eliza Poldern doesn't like them."

"Laura thinks that someone is interested in all the towers," said Rose, and Laura blushed vividly.

"I expect it was a silly idea," she mumbled.

"Why?" asked Lelant. "We thought the same, but—"

"Shut up, idiot!" hissed Isaac.

No one else seemed to be paying attention to the young ones, but Laura felt momentarily uneasy. She had seen them approaching the tower on the North Cliff. If there was any danger they shouldn't be involved.

"She doesn't know why," said Rose. "Do you, Laura?"

"Oh, it's those young people making sure there'll be dry places to sleep if the weather breaks," said Mrs.

Tregarth, pushing back her untidy hair as she rose from the table. "Never mind the school bus this morning, Lellie. I'll take you into Bodmin. I've some shopping to do. Anyone else want to come? Laura?"

Laura said she'd like to go, and Lelant rushed off to find her satchel and put on her school coat and hat. She attended a private school in Bodmin, while Isaac went to school in Trepoldern. Both children looked different that morning.

"But no school on May Day!" said Isaac, and went off, whistling.

Rose was wandering dreamily around the courtyard as Mrs. Tregarth drove away.

"That poor girl!" she murmured to Laura, who was in the front beside her. "Peter Poldern is a nice young man; I've known him all his life. But when he went away he only proved to me what I'd felt for some years. A slightly unsettled boy, unsure what he wanted from life. Rose is so deep. Warm-hearted and basically the kind of girl who needs to settle in her own place. I could have kicked Peter for not seeing her qualities."

"If she loved him she should have gone all out to get him," said the child in the back. "But I expect she was too proud."

Her mother said something under her breath as she swung the car into the streets of Trepoldern.

"Little pitchers have big ears!" she added aloud. "What can you know about it, at eleven? I didn't even know you'd guessed."

"I didn't. I heard you talking to Father. And then I

knew I'd been stupid. She always looked at him as if he was the only person in the world. If he doesn't love her now, I hate him!" said Lelant fiercely.

"Be quiet, Lellie. I should have held my tongue. We can't interfere. What will be will be. I'm talking in clichés," she ended ruefully. "George would laugh."

When they returned at eleven-thirty, Rose was ablaze with barely suppressed joy. They were all invited to dinner again at Poldern Place that evening. Looking at her, Laura could hardly remember the girl she had known in London.

Elvan wasn't in for lunch. He and Arthur had gone fishing again just for an hour or two, then he was meeting someone in St. Austell. After the meal Laura drifted down into the town, and found it a little more lively with the shops open and the people going about their daily business.

After a while she climbed the path to the North Cliff, went past the tower and climbed the stone stile. She noticed that, while the path she and Rose had taken went straight ahead, a second one, not as wide, dropped in a curve between gorse bushes, and she thought it might lead her quite quickly to the river bank.

So she went that way, enchanted by the nutty fragrance of the gorse, which grew more and more thickly. The path was rough and wound a good deal, and as she turned a corner, she suddenly stopped. Ahead, with his back to her, was Mr. Summer. There was no mistaking that straggly grey hair and shabby raincoat. He was standing still, with his head a little bent, as though in deep thought.

Strange old man! Boring, too. Laura didn't want any more of his company, and in another moment he might look around and see her. Laura moved swiftly and silently on to a secondary path that disappeared among the gorse bushes on her right. It was horribly prickly at its narrowest, but she moved as quietly as she could, hoping to reach the river bank, which must be quite near. Rose had said there were little coves along the River Poldern and it would be pleasant to explore them.

Yes, here was the river, and immediately below her, high black rocks and small patches of silvery sand. Laura sat down on the top of the sloping bank, dangling her feet. In another moment she had slithered quietly down on to the sand.

It had seemed a totally deserted place, with not even a boat on the water, but suddenly she was aware of voices. They came from behind the barrier of rocks.

Voices. . . . Well, one was only a sibilant whisper, but the other suddenly rose angrily.

"It's a mug's game! We're getting nowhere. That is, if you're telling me the truth. I wouldn't put it past you to doublecross me!"

The sibilant whisper came urgently, apparently denying the charge. The clearer voice went on:

"You said it'd be so easy. Find those cups and get out. But I'm more and more convinced it's a fool's errand. Hardly any clues. . . . Only the towers and that bit about—" Laura wasn't quite sure about the last few words, but they sounded like "the singing stone."

She crouched there, stiff with shock and incredulous interest. *Cups?* The Poldern cups?

The second voice had answered, still too low to hear. Then the louder voice went on:

"Yes, I do want to make some money. I'm darn sick of having none. But if you ask me, we haven't a cat's chance in hell."

Even the voice Laura could hear was unpleasant and husky. It was a rough voice . . . Cockney, perhaps; or, she thought, Australian speech was very like Cockney. But it wasn't Arthur Pengwern; of that she was certain. Besides, what could Arthur know about the missing Poldern cups? He had said that they might turn up, but he had seemed to be mocking the old story. She hadn't thought he was really interested.

Even the clearer voice had now dropped so low that she couldn't make out any words. Then it said impatiently, on a rising note: "Of course it's dangerous to meet, but I had to know if you'd made any progress. That's why I risked those few words as we passed each other in the town. Yes, well, May Day may be the best time. Everyone will be gathered near the hoss." There was a little more that Laura couldn't catch, then: "Better go now. You first. Oh, it's safe enough. I checked the rocks and bushes when I came."

There was the scrabbling sound of feet on the bank. Laura ducked down in terror of being seen. There wasn't much chance of it, as the bushes grew almost to the edge of the bank, and almost without thinking of it, she had crawled into a corner amongst the rocks. But say the second person checked again? She'd be in danger for certain. There had been something about that harsh, penetrating murmur that had been very frightening.

Yet, at the same time, curiosity and excitement filled her. She had to *know* who had been meeting on that lonely part of the river bank. It began to seem as if the mystery of the Poldern cups was not finished, after all. In fact, there were probably not two mysteries, but only one. But how on earth was she going to manage to see them without being discovered?

She lay huddled on the damp sand, and fumed, knowing that she dare not move until the second man had gone. Well, they must both have been men, though the other whisper had all the time been indistinct.

Several minutes passed and then she heard faint sounds as feet searched for footholds on the bank. A body brushed the gorse and then there was complete silence, except for the crying of a gull. Up toward the river mouth there were a few boats, but nearer at hand the shining water was still empty.

Fate, in the shape of Mr. Summer, had sent her to within a few feet of that secret meeting place, and the miracle was that they had not heard her approach. Say she had jumped down the bank? Her breathing quickened at the very thought.

It was maddening, but she knew that she dare not hurry back to the wider path. In fact, she'd do better to give up all hope of seeing them and make her way back along the shore, which looked quite possible now that the tide was going out. Fear of the unknown men was, after all, stronger than curiosity.

By the time she was struggling around the last of the rocks, finding herself within a few yards of some old boat sheds behind the North Quay, the whole episode was taking on the qualities of a dream and she was seriously doubting if her ears had heard aright. "The cups"—Yes, she had certainly heard that. And they had mentioned the towers and a singing stone. Singing sands there were, in some places, but never a singing stone. That much was certainly nonsense. And who would believe her if she told the story? Yet it was evidence that she had been right about the towers.

The Trepoldern police? But she had already seen two of the three. They were slow-looking, youngish men, with soft Cornish voices, and they seemed to spend some of their time, at least, placidly gossiping. She doubted if they would spring into action if a strange girl went to them with her wild tale. They were too young to have any very definite memories of the theft and murder of twenty years ago. They would have been boys of ten or thereabouts at the time, and of course they might not even be natives of the town.

Laura sat on a seat on the quay and continued musing. The affair had been in the hands of Scotland Yard, but would they come down on what might be a wild goose chase? In any case, everyone would soon know, and then the mysterious searchers would be warned.

It would be wonderful for the Polderns if the cups

turned up again. They could be sold, and the money used for the estate and to refurbish the shabby but beautiful old house. So should she tell Mr. Poldern in confidence?

"Mr. Poldern, I heard voices. . . ." Just like Joan of Arc. How awful if he laughed! For he didn't know her, none of them really knew her, and they might well think she was carried away by the romance of Cornwall and the old stories.

Eventually she went on into the town, and there she saw Arthur at the wheel of a very old car. At first he seemed to be frowning heavily, but when he saw her he smiled and drew up.

"Well, hi! Jump in and see how she goes. I thought I'd take her along that road to the river mouth. I hear there's a cove and a big cave."

"I've been there," Laura said. "Rose and I walked along the cliff path. Not now, I'm sorry."

He was looking at her closely.

"What's the matter? You look upset."

"Of course I'm not." He couldn't have been that other whisper, though he would have had plenty of time to get down off the cliff and fetch the car. "I have to get back, that's all. The car looks very nice."

Turning away she almost cannoned into Isaac, apparently just out of school. The little boy stared after the old car.

"Where'd he get that?"

"He's just bought it for next to nothing," Laura explained.

"Yes, it belonged to one of the shopkeepers. D'you like Arthur Pengwern?"

"I don't know," said Laura cautiously.

"Lellie and I hate him. He *kicked* poor Bill. We were on the road one day and he didn't know we'd seen. Bill was just being friendly. Are you going back to tea?"

Laura nodded, and Isaac said:

"Coming in a minute. Just want to see a friend." And he ran off.

By the time Laura reached the courtyard she had more or less decided to tell Elvan what had happened by the river, and see what he said. All the same arguments applied, and she certainly didn't want him to think her a silly young fool. But there was just a chance he'd believe her and offer to help. She couldn't keep it entirely to herself, and if Elvan would tell Mr. Pengwern. . . .

To tell or not. To be or not to be. . . . Oh, bother!

Instead of going in search of tea, she sat on a stone in a sheltered corner of the courtyard, with a cat on her knee, and frowned at the house. And, while she still sat there, Elvan drove into the courtyard and drew up within a few yards of her.

Laura rose to her feet and then saw, with shock, that his brows were drawn together in a heavy frown. He gave her only the briefest of nods and strode off into the house.

Rebuffed and frightened, Laura stared after him. He had looked a different person from the one who had laughed and sung the previous evening, from the young man who had stood with her on the hill's edge, gazing down at the quiet port.

Very slowly she followed Elvan into the house. The mystery suddenly seemed unimportant. She wondered why he had looked like that, and, because she was already in love, she thought that it must be something to do with her.

9. *Which of the Strangers?*

"What in the world is the matter with Elvan?" Mrs. Tregarth asked as she, Rose and Laura lingered in the living room after tea. George Tregarth was not yet home and the children had run off together. Elvan had drunk two cups of tea without saying a word, and had then departed.

"What?" Rose asked vaguely.

Her mother gave her a faintly exasperated look.

"Well, something's happened to upset him. Perhaps he didn't have a very pleasant lunch in St. Austell for some reason. It was something to do with his work. The meeting had been arranged before he decided to take a holiday. He was as nearly rude as I've ever seen him."

He hadn't even looked at Laura. She still had the terrible feeling that she might have offended him, but she told herself that that was nonsense. He had been his usual self at breakfast time.

"There did seem to be something wrong," she ventured.

"Well, I hope he finds his social manners before dinner. It won't be much of a homecoming for Peter if Elvan has nothing to say. They were good friends in the old days."

Laura didn't see Elvan again until she emerged from her room, ready to go to Poldern Place. By then she had recovered her spirits a little, because really life was too exciting to allow herself to be miserable. Whatever was worrying Elvan surely wouldn't last long. As she dressed she had looked across at Poldern Place and thought of Peter already home, and of the long ago night when the precious cups had been stolen.

When she stepped out into the corridor there was Elvan, still frowning, but apparently again aware of her existence.

"I'll take you over, Laura," he said.

The two cars went slowly out of the courtyard and down the narrow road, and from the top of the tower, the two children watched them.

"I do think it's mean not to ask *us!*" Isaac grumbled.

"Never mind, we can do a little investigating after supper. It'll be light for ages," Lelant remarked.

"What can we do? They might see us if we went up to the Poldern Place tower."

"We can keep our eyes and ears open," Lelant said. "We'll go into the town and watch the strangers."

"But we haven't anything to go on," the boy pointed out. "Someone interested in towers, looking for something, perhaps. Treasure, the way they do in books. But there isn't any treasure in Trepoldern."

"There might be," said Lelant dreamily. "There was

great treasure. You've heard the story hundreds of times from all kinds of people. And some do believe they're still here."

Isaac's face brightened.

"You mean the Poldern Cups? Oh, but they were lost in the dark ages. Years and years ago. No one will find them now."

"Twenty years ago," said his sister. "It is a long time, of course. Only Elvan was born. And they weren't ever found and they might be still here. Think if *we* could find them. They were beautiful; golden with jewels. Perhaps King Arthur drank out of them. They're the only things anyone *could* be looking for."

Isaac frowned.

"But we don't know for sure anyone's looking for anything. Though there does seem to be a mystery; Laura thought so, too."

"Well, even if no one is, *we* can look. And the towers give us a start. But we can watch the strangers at the same time. All those peculiar young ones, and then there are some others. Mr. Summer—"

"Oh, him!" Isaac snorted. "He's crazy!"

"Hum! He does behave oddly. No harm in watching him. He's staying at the Ship. Who else is there?"

"Arthur Pengwern," said her brother.

"Oh, but he belongs to the Vicarage. I don't like him, but still—"

"I know you're up there, me dears!" shouted Bess's voice. "Come on down. Your supper's getting cold."

The children scrambled down the tower steps.

"Anyway, it will give us something exciting to do," said Lelant. "What a pity we have to go to school!"

And so the two youngest Tregarths were already on the fringe of the mystery.

During the short drive to Poldern Place Elvan scarcely spoke a word. As they passed through the gates and saw the long frontage of the house, with its flanking tower, Laura thought again of the whispering voices and the old mystery. This family had a history that went back into distant centuries. It was a far cry from her own modern, cheerful home on the Dee marshes to this family that had owned a castle maybe tied up with King Arthur. Could it really be that the ancient cups were still lying hidden in Trepoldern?

Then they joined Mr. and Mrs. Tregarth and Rose on the gravel sweep in front of the porch, and for a moment Laura touched Rose's cold hand. Then the door was opened and the Polderns were all in the hall to greet them. Peter Poldern, a big young man, handsome and broad shouldered, came forward. He kissed Rose on the cheek and Laura's heart beat faster for her friend's carefully checked emotion. Rose looked—well, if Peter was blind to that he was beyond hope.

It was a strange evening, though in many ways it repeated the pattern of the former occasion. The strangeness lay in Laura's own knowledge and awareness. Her very skin seemed sensitive to atmosphere. To Rose's feelings as they sat at the candle-lit table; to Elvan, making what was clearly an effort at social pleasantries. But the evening was saved by Peter Poldern's evident delight in his return. It was he who talked, telling about his experiences, but he made it clear that he was staying in Cornwall now.

He was, he said, going to take over one of the farms and settle down. If there was a girl somewhere she was only a ghost at that dinner party. He sat between Rose and Laura and paid equal attention to each, but Laura heard him murmur, as they rose from the table:

"I missed you, Rose dear. They told me you'd gone to work in London. I suppose you're much too sophisticated for Cornwall now?"

Rose's reply was inaudible.

"You didn't ask Arthur this time," remarked Elvan, as they drank their coffee in the drawing-room.

Mrs. Poldern shook her head.

"It's a family occasion, and you Tregarths almost count as family. That young man's such a bore; so uncouth. I feel sorry for him, stuck with the Vicar and his wife, but I suppose he came here of his own free will."

"May Day, perhaps," said her husband. "He wouldn't be the first to be drawn back across the world. The tune—"

"Maybe, though he didn't seem to have much feeling for the Festival. I expect the fact that he was adopted by the Australian side of his family made a difference to his attitude."

Laura couldn't help feeling out of the family occasion, though she had seemed to be accepted so naturally. But now she asked with sudden boldness:

Which of the Strangers?   95

"Did Arthur's father go away before the cups were stolen?"

There was a surprised silence, then Mr. Poldern said:

"Must have done. Well, twenty years. . . . Yes, of course."

Arthur had said twenty-four years, but she had wanted to make sure. In any case, his father had been the Vicar's son and wouldn't, surely, have turned thief and murderer! She nearly said, "Mr. Poldern, I heard voices on the shore." But there was no reason at all to suspect Arthur, and she could just imagine their polite disbelief if she came out with the story.

So the evening passed and Laura was back in the old car with Elvan. Whatever his mood, she was determinedly treasuring every moment. Two weeks were so terribly short, and if they were all she was ever going to have then she must make the best of them. But she was astonished when he turned down to the harbor, instead of driving straight back to the castle.

He parked on the deserted quay, turned to her and asked:

"Why did you want to know about Arthur Pengwern's father?"

Laura was unable to speak for a moment. This was her chance, but she was suddenly afraid. Oh, he would laugh! Not that he had laughed once that evening.

"I just wondered."

"My turn to ask if *you* like him?"

"No-o. But in a way I'm sorry for him. He admitted

to me that his grandparents are getting him down. And he has almost no money and will have to get some kind of job."

"Well, without meaning to be uncharitable, they are a tiresome old pair. The Vicar is a wordy old bore and his wife a querulous invalid, usually bedridden. But that doesn't explain your interest in his father and the theft of the Poldern cups."

"He can't have had anything to do with it, I know," Laura said slowly. "But something happened today. . . . I have to tell someone. Only I'm so afraid you'll laugh."

"I promise not to," said Elvan gravely. "You'd better explain."

"Then I'd better start at the beginning—" And Laura haltingly told her suspicions about the towers, and went on to describe her experience on the shore and the words she had overheard.

"I never really heard the other voice, but the one I did hear wasn't Arthur Pengwern. I'm sure of that, though it might have been Australian, or Cockney. It certainly wasn't Cornish. The other one *could* have been Arthur, I suppose, though I don't see how he or anyone else would get such slight clues about the whereabouts of the cups. If they're still hidden here the person who did it must know exactly where. I've just grown suspicious of all the strangers," she ended lamely, and waited nervously for his comments.

Elvan was silent for several moments.

"I'm far from laughing. I don't like the sound of it at all. You were probably in great danger. You're *sure* that the two who were talking had no real idea where the cups might be?"

"It sounded like that. I've told you exactly what I heard. The only clue was the towers, he said, and then something that sounded like the 'singing stone.' Only that must have been wrong, of course. Could it have been a place name or a surname? Swinson or Shilling-stone, and my ears played tricks?"

"I can't think of anywhere or anyone with a name like that," Elvan said slowly.

"Ought we to tell someone, do you think? I decided that the police here would be hopeless, and there's so little to go on."

"Not yet. I agree with you it's all too vague." Then Elvan added suddenly: "We'd better get back. They'll think we're lost. Now remember, Laura, don't do anything rash. Try to forget it. I'll think it over and see if there's anything I can do."

"But it's *my* mystery!" Laura protested. "I was scared this afternoon, but I won't be left out." She was slightly nettled by his commanding tone and for a moment almost forgot that she wanted to please him.

They stared at each other in the dim light, faintly hostile, and then Elvan laughed and touched her hand.

"I can see you're obstinate, but those cups are beyond price. And remember, someone attacked old Joseph. If the old chap hadn't had a thick skull he might have died."

"Yes, I'll be careful, but I'm interested and I can't forget it. There must be more to find out."

Elvan turned the car and drove away from the harbor. As they passed the opening to the North Quay they saw a row of the raffish strangers sitting on an old boat. One was twanging a banjo, and the sound came through the open window of the car in a melancholy way, born on the chilly spring wind.

"It must be cold up on the headland," Elvan remarked. "How many of them are there so far? Twenty or more, I should think. It would make good cover, I suppose, but, as you said, the most mysterious thing of all is how anyone would get a clue about the Poldern Cups without knowing exactly where they are. Yes, and they're all too young to know anything at first hand.

"The strangers. . . . Yes, and so is Arthur Pengwern. If we could find out who they are—those two you heard talking—they might lead us to the cups. And I wouldn't mind helping to restore that treasure to the Polderns. Apart from anything else, they're part of the historic treasure of England and oughtn't to be hidden somewhere where they might be damaged by damp."

"You really believe it!" Laura cried, in relief and astonishment. There was also somewhere in her mind a feeling of warm amusement. A scientist, was he, and four or five years older? But there was a ring in his voice that spoke of a longing for adventure and achievement.

"Well, the thing was never solved, but whoever took them wouldn't dare to turn up himself. He was a murderer, remember."

"I suppose he might never have left Trepoldern."

"Well, yes. But in that case, surely he'd have taken

them away as soon as the uproar died down? Within a few years, anyway. That may have happened, even. But I know all the towers. There's nowhere anything might be hidden in ours or in the one on the North Cliff. I should doubt it in the one at Poldern Place. And would the thief take time to hide the cups so near the house, when the murder and theft might have been discovered at any minute? The church tower seems the most likely."

"Would the church be open in the middle of the night?" Laura asked, frowning intently. They had driven into the courtyard and Elvan had turned off the lights. As they got out of the car he said:

"It might have been in those days. We could ask the Vicar. They might have thought it safe enough then. Not so many petty criminals and hoodlums around."

"Only murderers, apparently."

"You have a point there; but no one was expecting that kind of violence."

"Arthur Pengwern was coming out of the tower," Laura said suddenly.

"When? The church tower? How do you know?"

"I saw him. I was with Mr. Summer. I couldn't shake him off. I'd met him at the lookout tower, and, for some reason, I told him I thought someone was interested in towers. When we got into the church the tower door was ajar and we pushed it open and stood talking. After a few moments Arthur came down. He had a camera and said he'd been taking pictures of the Vicarage from the top."

"Well, he could have been. He's interested in unusual angles. I've seen him practically standing on his head to take photographs of the boats in the harbor. What about Mr. Summer, though, Laura? He's a stranger, when all's said and done, and a pretty odd one. All that folklore business could be a cover."

"Oh, but he must know something about folklore, or your father would have spotted it. He's just a bumbling old idiot."

"Yet you said he was there. That was why you ducked into the gorse and went down to the river."

"Oh!" said Laura, very blankly indeed.

"He could have been on his way to the meetingplace arranged by your Cockney-Australian friend. There are plenty of narrow paths over there. You went one way and he could have gone another."

"I suppose he could. I went slowly and it was lucky I did. He's old, but he can move quite fast."

"Well, I think Mr. Summer could be investigated. I'll get to know him better. I'll—"

"You two staying out there all night?" demanded Bess's voice, and they jumped guiltily.

"No. It's cold. We were just talking. Come on in, Laura."

Once more Laura took a long time to get to sleep. She and Elvan seemed joined in a conspiracy; he would try to keep her out, but it wasn't going to be easy for him to do that. Certainly there might be some danger, but she would be very careful. If there was the faintest chance of the cups being returned to the Polderns she wanted to have a hand in their recovery.

She was practically asleep at last when she jerked awake again. For she realized suddenly that she still had no idea what had upset Elvan that day. He had gone fishing for a while with Arthur and later had lunch in St. Austell. It *must* have been something said during lunch. Could he even have been meeting the girl Rose had mentioned, and they had quarreled? Life seemed full of secrets and puzzles, but, on the whole, she found it exciting and satisfying.

In the morning, when the children and George Tregarth had gone, the others lingered at the breakfast table. The telephone rang and Bess announced that the Vicar wanted to speak to Mrs. Tregarth. She came back to say that Rose and Laura were invited to lunch at the Vicarage.

"Oh, I can't! I'm going out with Peter," Rose said quickly. "He asked me to go for a drive and have lunch in Penzance or somewhere. I'm awfully sorry, Laura. I'm neglecting you."

"I'll go with Laura," said Elvan.

His mother looked pleased, but astonished.

"But you'll loathe it. The food will be terrible and that dreadful old housekeeper of theirs grumbles all the time. It's difficult, but I could say that both girls have a previous engagement."

"Oh, better get it over with!" Elvan said lightly. "They'll meet Laura, and Rose can drop in later. We'll support each other, won't we, Laura?"

"Then I'll tell the Vicar. Rose will certainly have to

see them soon, but Mrs. Pengwern dotes on you, Elvan."
And his mother went back to the telephone.

"But why did you want to come?" Laura asked, meeting Elvan half an hour later. "If it's about whether the church could have been open or not I suppose I could manage to ask tactfully."

Elvan grinned, and she remembered that she had thought his eyebrows Puckish.

"I thought you might like my company."

Laura blushed vividly, but he had already gone past her and it didn't matter. She thought he must have another reason, but she didn't much care at that moment. Certainly she would like his company. It promised to be another exciting day, even with the prospect of bad food and a grumbling housekeeper at the Vicarage.

10. *Elvan in Danger*

Elvan and Laura walked to the Vicarage. When they had passed through the little square and turned the corner toward Church Lane, the first person they saw was Mr. Summer.

The unusually fine weather had made some of the inns and little restaurants put tables out in the open air, and there, outside The Cornish Cream, sat the folklorist, drinking coffee with two of the unkempt strangers. One was the large, dirty young man with the curly beard, and the other was smaller, with shifty eyes and a violent orange sweater. He, too, seemed to be a musician, for two guitars were propped up against the restaurant window.

Mr. Summer hailed Elvan and Laura with delight.

"Good morning! And a very fine morning it is. What a very charming pair you make!"

Laura blushed and Orange Sweater laughed in rather an objectionable way.

"Thank you very much," Elvan said, with commendable gravity. "I hope you're enjoying your stay here?"

"Oh, most certainly, though I could wish that the local people were more friendly and outgoing—as I believe the Americans say. They are so secretive about their Great Horse. But on May Day we shall all take part. I look forward to singing the song. Believe me, I shall be there when the proceedings open. Outside the Great Horse Inn, I understand, when the clock strikes midnight."

"Yes, that's when we sing the Night Song. The hoss doesn't come out until ten-thirty the next morning."

"How very exciting it will be! I've just visited your charming Vicar and come away with a flea in my ear, as the expressive saying goes. He gave me to understand that he doesn't approve of pagan festivals in his parish. Yet, as I pointed out, the Church, in many cases, smiled on such things and even managed to draw them under the hem of Christianity. The horns are kept in the church at Abbots Bromley, for instance—"

"Mr. Pengwern is a stuffy old thing, I'm afraid," Elvan remarked. "Very much the old school. I'm sorry he was rude."

"Hardly rude. Just obstructive. One gets used to it in my work."

"Probably stays out of the way on May Day," said Orange Sweater.

"We might have another talk, sir," said Elvan politely. "I was born here. I met the horse when I was a baby."

"I should be delighted!"

Elvan was frowning as he and Laura walked up Church Lane.

"He can't be genuine. It's impossible!"

"I suppose there are people like that," said Laura.

"Well, yes. We've had 'em before. I wonder what he's doing with those two?"

"He said he was interested in them. Perhaps they're nearer to simple things."

"Simple? That lot? In spite of what I said to Father, I should think they're all drug-takers. I've taken a better look at them."

The Vicarage loomed up before them, elegant in its Georgian simplicity. Laura was suddenly shy and nervous.

"Elvan, why *did* you come? If it's Arthur—"

Elvan laughed. He seemed in better spirits that morning.

"I have my reasons. But don't worry."

They were received by a very old woman in a dusty black dress. The Vicar and Arthur were in an old-fashioned drawing room, drinking sherry. Arthur looked out of place in the room.

The Vicar, a very thin, aesthetic-looking man, greeted Laura effusively.

"How do you do, my dear? A friend of the Tregarths', of dear Rose! We are, I gather, to have the pleasure of seeing Rose later. My wife is bedridden, but hopes to meet you after lunch. Sherry?"

Elvan accepted sherry. Laura asked for a fruit drink.

She was oppressed by the room, which was heavy with ugly Victorian furniture. Arthur seemed restless and ill at ease, and Elvan was the only one who seemed really calm and natural.

"Such a tiresome morning," the Vicar said, handing drinks. "That terrible old man! Solomon Summer, he said his name was. Seemed to think I'd be willing to talk to him about May Day. 'My dear sir,' I said, 'I've spent fifty years ignoring the horse.' I came here as a curate, of course. My mother was Cornish, but she was too intelligent a woman to believe in old superstitions. I had hoped to use my influence, but alas—"

"The May Day festivities are surely very innocent, sir," Elvan said lightly. "They bring everyone together in the best possible way. No quarrels remembered on May Day—"

"You are right, up to a point. At all events, they cling to it. Oh, is lunch ready, Hannah? Then we'll go in."

Lunch was certainly a dreadful meal, badly cooked and served. Laura was increasingly sorry for Arthur, but he ate the horrible food with an appearance of gusto.

On the way down the hill from the castle they had agreed not to ask about the locking of the church door in front of Arthur, but, when they were just finishing their coffee, fate was kind. The old curate arrived and it seemed that Arthur had offered to help move a heavy chest in the church.

"So useful having a strong young man about the place," said the Vicar. "And while you're away, Arthur, Laura must meet your grandmother."

Arthur went off and Elvan rose firmly with Laura.

"I haven't seen Mrs. Pengwern for a long time, so—"

"Of course, my dear boy. Go up. You know the way? I have some letters to write."

Elvan paused at the foot of the stairs.

"I was wondering if the church door is locked at night, sir?"

The Vicar looked surprised.

"It most certainly is. It may not be Christian, but I never trust strangers, especially these very peculiar types we are unfortunate enough to attract at the moment. For some years, actually, I have locked it every night at eight o'clock, unless, for some reason, the church is being used."

"But I suppose it was left open quite safely in the... in the distant past?"

The Vicar looked more surprised than ever.

"Now that is a most extraordinary thing! Really most extraordinary! My visitor this morning, Mr. Summer, asked the very same question."

Laura choked, and Elvan coughed. But he remained calm.

"Yes, that is strange. But he's so interested in the past. Well, we'll go and pay our respects to Mrs. Pengwern."

"But—" Laura muttered, as they went up the stairs.

"Not now. Just be social. Take no notice of anything I do."

Mrs. Pengwern lay in a big bed, with a lunch tray pushed aside on the table beside it. She greeted Laura with avid curiosity, asking many questions. Where did she live? Alone in London? Was that wise when she was such a young girl? She had always thought that Rose's father should have refused to let her go.

Elvan wandered around the room. There were a great many plants on the window sill, and somehow he managed to knock over an unpleasant-looking cactus. Apologizing profusely, he shoveled the soil back with his hands.

Mrs. Pengwern watched him fretfully.

"Oh, never mind! It can be thrown out. I hate that plant. But your hands . . . you must go and wash. You know where the bathroom is?"

"Of course. I'm so sorry," said Elvan and vanished.

Laura talked on, feverishly, for a few minutes. She knew that Elvan was up to something, but couldn't imagine what. Footsteps on the stairs, then the old housekeeper saying:

"Did you want something in Mr. Arthur's room, Mr. Tregarth?"

"No, just borrowing his comb. I forgot mine and when I was washing my hands I saw I looked untidy. I'm very sorry, Hannah, but I upset a plant in your mistress's room."

Hannah came in, grumbling, and removed the plant. Elvan, following on her heels, looked rather flushed, but still calm. A few minutes later they got themselves out of the room, and, in the hall, met Arthur.

"I have my uses," Arthur said, grinning. "Oh, don't go! Oh, well, if you must. . . . But how about going fishing again in the morning?"

"I'll ring you," Elvan said. "I may be going to the

farm. We'll just say good-bye to the Vicar."

Out in Church Lane, Laura could hardly wait.

"What were you doing in Arthur's room? You made the opportunity on purpose, didn't you?"

Elvan looked at her, smiling a little.

"I had my reasons."

"Oh!" For a moment Laura could have hit him. She loved him—oh, yes, she loved him very much, however silly it might be—but he really could be irritating! "Were you looking for something? Do you really suspect Arthur?"

"Well," said Elvan evasively, "we said we more or less suspected all the strangers, didn't we? I thought I'd just take a look at his papers.... Passport, you know, and anything else I could find."

"And did you find his passport?"

"Oh, yes, at once. Under some underclothes in a drawer. All present and correct, though I only had a glimpse. I heard the old girl coming."

"But I don't see what you wanted to prove from his passport. Now Mr. Summer seems another matter. Fancy him asking about the church door being locked in the past!"

"Yes, that is fishy," Elvan admitted. "He *could* have been your second voice. But we're looking for a possible Australian as well, aren't we? Arthur said he heard about the theft of the cups as a child, and other Trepoldern people might have also. Groups of them stuck together in Australia, I believe. There are a lot at some town in the Outback. Desert Springs, or something like that. In the meantime, I think I'll loaf around and find Mr. Summer."

"I want to loaf, too," Laura said boldly.

Elvan laughed.

"I know. It's your mystery. But I'd prefer to keep you out of any danger. Oh, well, come on. We'll look and listen. You might recognize that voice again."

The oddly dressed and often dirty strangers seemed everywhere, but they appeared harmless enough. If they noticed the suspicious scowls of the local people they were determinedly ignoring them.

"I think there are more of them than yesterday," said Laura, as they strolled along the narrow street that led to the harbor.

"I believe you're right. It does complicate things. Now where on earth is our friend Mr. Summer?"

It was an hour before they chanced on him, and then he was sitting alone on an upturned boat on the North Quay. He looked pleased to see them.

"How delightful! I have been exploring . . . so much to see. But at my age one quickly grows tired. I do so wish more people would talk to me. I have a natural sympathy for folk who make their lives in remote places. Life can't be easy here. Not much work, and few prospects for young people."

"No. That's why so many Trepoldern people went away over the years. I'll tell you some of my memories of the hoss, if you like," Elvan offered. And he talked for quite a while, so well and vividly that Laura almost forgot the mystery in her own deep interest. She presently noticed with surprise that Mr. Summer did not seem to be paying very much attention.

Catching her eye, he suddenly coughed and sat up more alertly on the boat.

"So fascinating! Really you have enlightened me very much," he said quickly to Elvan.

"I hope you'll find your visit rewarding in the end," Elvan said politely.

"I certainly hope so," agreed the folklorist. "I have meant to come for some years, but I'm busy and there are other events on May Day. You are a scientist, I believe your father told me. How does that tie up with pagan rites?"

"It doesn't," Elvan admitted. "But I wouldn't miss May Day. I suppose you've met Trepoldern people away from here. Perhaps in London?"

"Never, alas. I first read about the Festival of the Great Horse in one of your father's excellent books."

"We try to avoid publicity. Father wasn't too popular when he wrote about May Day. But sometimes we get publicity in other ways. There was the affair of the Poldern cups; I was only a small child then. You'll have heard about it?"

Mr. Summer looked vague.

"I think not. Cups? Were they won for something?"

"No, they were medieval cups in the possession of the Poldern family. They were stolen and never recovered."

"Most interesting," said Mr. Summer, in perfunctory tones. "A local mystery. But my whole mind, such as it is, is given to more ancient matters."

"All the same," said Laura, as she and Elvan walked back to the castle, "he didn't seem very interested in what you were telling him about the horse."

"I noticed that, too," Elvan agreed. "He tried, but he looked as if his thoughts were far away. Perhaps he really is just old and vague."

"And perhaps he knows more about the cups than he admits," said Laura.

When they reached the castle they found that old Joseph was back. He was a small, wiry man of seventy-five, with a cheerful face and the rolling gait of a sailor.

"Told you I'd be back for May Day, didn't I?" he greeted Elvan. "Those darn doctors made such a fuss about a crack on the head. Daft as brushes, the lot of 'em. I hear they never got the chap that did it?"

"The police had no clues," said Elvan.

"Aye, that's a pity. I saw nothing. Not a darn thing." He had been eyeing Laura with appreciation and Elvan introduced them.

"Miss Edmund is from London, Joe."

"And pretty as a picture! Now isn't that nice, me dear? You here for May Day, and me back where I belong in time to tease the hoss."

"He's no help at all," said Elvan, as he and Laura went indoors. "But I think Mr. Summer might be worth a little more watching. I'm going down to the Ship for a drink tonight."

Rose came home at teatime, flushed and dazed-looking. Not exactly happy; certainly not miserable. Laura hoped she'd be told something about Peter, but was not. That evening George Tregarth suggested dinner in Newquay, so that Laura could see the town, but Elvan excused himself. Laura wished very much that she could have gone to the Ship Inn, too. Her mind was much on the mystery, but she tried to enjoy herself.

Elvan ate supper with the children, then read for a while. It was sunset when he rose and put on his coat. The evening was very still and he walked slowly down into the town. As he went he turned over the various mysterious happenings in his mind. Laura's eager face intruded a good deal. He had known very well that she would have preferred to go to the Ship with him. The place was a perfectly respectable residential inn and she *could* have gone. But he had a curious certainty of danger. It wasn't only the Great Horse that was brooding in Trepoldern, waiting for May Day. Something was afoot, and there had been some violence done already. Pretty young girls from London had to be kept out of it as much as possible. He hadn't even told Laura *his* side of the story, the thing he thought he had discovered the previous day. And that seemed to have been wrong, anyway.

Thinking thus, he came down into the town and turned toward the harbor. Turning a corner near the square he almost ran into his small brother and sister. They had a conspiratorial air and looked guilty as they stepped back.

"You're not supposed to be down here so late," said

Elvan. "Bess thought you were up on the tower. Where have you been?"

"Nowhere. We're not babies now," Lelant said coldly.

"Well, Isaac's only nine and you aren't so mature yourself," her brother retorted. "I don't like it with all these strangers around. Get on up the hill at the double."

"Yes, Elvan," they agreed meekly, and ran off.

"They'd been up to something," Elvan thought, as he walked around the harbor to the Ship Inn. "Bess has little authority over them these days."

The public bar at the Ship was crowded, both with locals and strangers. Elvan ordered himself a beer and sat in a corner, looking out for Mr. Summer. He had already looked in the residents' lounge and not found him. He sat there for quite a while, keeping his ears open and scarcely touching his drink.

He was just telling himself that he had come on a wild goose chase when Mr. Summer entered the bar. He was not alone. He had a youngish man with him, dressed in city clothes. There were two seats at Elvan's table and they came over to join him. Mr. Summer seemed quite pleased to see him.

"This is Mr. Jones, a journalist from London," he said, introducing the other man. "He only arrived today and we got talking over dinner. So very pleasant to have company."

It didn't take Elvan long to decide that Mr. Jones was genuine. He worked, he explained, for a daily paper, and someone had suggested there might be a story in the Festival. The bar was smoky and increasingly crowded and Elvan finally decided to call it a night and go home. He'd learned nothing and might just as well have gone with the others.

It was quite dark as he walked back around the harbor. The sky was starry, though, and there was a young moon. The clear cold air was very welcome after the heat of the inn, and he walked slowly, and very quietly, for his shoes had rubber soles. The center of the town was deserted, though he thought he saw two forms in the bus shelter.

Halfway up the hill to the castle he suddenly stopped, sure that there was someone behind him. He wasn't aware that he had heard any sound; it was more a primitive instinct that had warned him. But, in the silence of the night, he then heard a faint rattle, as of a loose stone displaced.

The moon had gone behind a cloud and it was pretty dark on the lonely road.

Elvan softly rounded a corner and stopped again. He heard another faint rattle, quite near. The road led nowhere but to the castle, so the natural assumption was that someone was following him. And, if he could find out who it was, it might go a long way toward solving the mystery.

Elvan was a big young man and very strong, and he felt himself quite able to cope with any attacker, provided he was warned. But he had time to remember Laura and be thankful that she was not with him.

He crouched in a waiting attitude against the bank and looked forward to the satisfaction of confronting the follower. But suddenly, up at the castle, there was the sound of barking. Bess had let the dogs out for their last run. The barking very rapidly came nearer, and Elvan cursed under his breath. The dogs were old, but they could still move, and they seemed to have scented him.

They certainly had! Two furry bodies hurtled against him. He tried to push them aside and Bill got between his legs. Elvan tripped and fell and felt a rough tongue licking his cheek.

"Oh, you darned nuisances!" he whispered, getting to his feet. For the stranger—well, the quiet follower—was going away. The dogs, pleased to find him, had now stopped barking, and he quite clearly heard the rattle of stones well down the hill.

"After him, boys!" he urged. But the dogs had already turned toward the castle. They had had their fun and were eager to go home.

Elvan followed them gloomily. He had lost his chance and might not have another as good. He was fairly sure that he had been in some danger of attack, but the follower might have been anyone. Arthur. . . . Laura's Cockney-Australian whisperer. . . . Mr. Summer. *Someone* might suspect that he was interested in what was going on in Trepoldern and think it better to put him out of action. The only other explanation was that he had been so quiet that someone had not known he was ahead. Twice there had been an intruder in their tower.

. . . Still, it was early for anyone to venture up to the castle.

When Elvan reached home the others were still not back. But they arrived within ten minutes, and found him reading in the living room. George Tregarth went to his study, Rose said she wanted nothing more to eat or drink and went to her room, and Mrs. Tregarth went to the kitchen to heat some milk for herself and Laura, and to make coffee for Elvan.

That left Laura with Elvan and she guessed at once that something had happened. Elvan told her briefly, making light of it.

"I was just so darn mad with the dogs for spoiling my chance," he said. "Don't say anything about it, Laura."

"Of course not. It's part of the mystery."

Laura went to bed feeling puzzled and rather troubled. She didn't like the thought of someone following Elvan in such a sinister way on the lonely road. More and more she was convinced that something dark and secret was going on in Trepoldern.

But, when she awoke to another bright morning, everywhere looked so quiet and beautiful that mystery and danger seemed unreal and unlikely. This was May Eve, she told herself, as she looked down at Trepoldern. At midnight she would be outside the Great Horse Inn, and May Day would begin!

Elvan telephoned Arthur and arranged to go fishing for a couple of hours. He told Laura he might as well, as his father didn't really need him at the farm.

Quite late in the morning Laura and Rose strolled

down into the town. Rose, suddenly articulate, poured out her feelings about Peter.

"Oh, in some ways it's wonderful, Laura. I'm so happy just to be with him I hardly know what to do or say. But he keeps on remarking that I must be too sophisticated for Cornwall now. How can I say I only went away because I missed him so much? I have to have some pride, but it's so hard not to express what I feel, and I can't be sure he—"

She talked on all the way to the North Quay, when they were suddenly startled to see a small crowd gathered. Two of the policemen were there, and Rose cried sharply:

"That's the boat Elvan and Arthur hired! Laura, look! I think something's happened to Elvan. He must be hurt. . . . He's holding his arm!"

They ran forward, pushing their way through the crowd.

"Someone shot him, he says, me dears," said an old fisherman. "Out in the boat fishing, they were. Might have been killed."

11. The Night Song

But he hadn't been killed, Laura assured herself, trying to control her breathing after the moments of sharp terror. In fact, Elvan looked very much alive, though a trickle of blood was running down his arm from under a knotted handkerchief.

Arthur was the one who looked all in. He was white, and beads of sweat stood out on his brow.

"But what exactly happened? Why should anyone shoot at the boat?" Rose elbowed aside the youngest policeman, whom Laura now knew to be called Bert Trelawney, and reached her brother.

"Someone tried to kill me!" Arthur said loudly.

"Kill *you?*" Laura asked, in surprise. The memory of the mysterious follower on the dark road last night leaped into her mind. Elvan *must* have been the target, though why she couldn't imagine. Unless someone thought he was a danger to secret plans—and, in that case, she might come under the same heading.

"We were fishing quite close inshore," Elvan was

explaining calmly. "Beyond the North Cliff, where all the bushes are." Briefly his eyes met Laura's. The bushes that she already knew well. "Arthur was in one end of the boat and I was in the other. The first shot whistled past Arthur's head and the second grazed my arm. It's nothing; just a slight flesh wound. So we flung ourselves flat in the boat and let her drift off on the tide until we were out of range."

"Someone shooting rabbits up there," said Bert Trelawney, in his slow way.

"With a revolver?" Arthur asked excitedly. "Well, that's what it sounded like. Not a shotgun."

"Oh, come, sir!" protested the second policeman, his usually placid face puzzled and troubled. "Now who would by lying up there with a revolver, waiting to shoot at a boat?"

"Not at a boat. At me!" said Arthur. Then he seemed to pull himself together. "No, of course I've no idea who it could be. That's your job. But whoever it was will have gone now."

The crowd had grown. Most of the unkempt strangers seemed to be there, and Mr. Summer was hovering at the back, his hands in his raincoat pockets. He looked mildly curious.

There was a good deal of whispering and argument among the inhabitants of Trepoldern.

"An accident, it must have been."

"Lucky it was no worse. Might have been nasty."

"Might have been more than nasty. One of this lot, I

wouldn't be surprised." And hostile glances were cast at the long-haired young men, who for once seemed uneasy.

"We don't carry guns," said Orange Sweater.

"Better go and see if the doctor's home, Mr. Tregarth," said Bert Trelawney. "Ought to have that wound looked at. We'll get right up to the cliff and see if we can spot anything, but like as not it was someone shooting at rabbits. Won't come forward and confess, that's certain."

"Yes, come on, Elvan," urged Rose, who still looked shaken.

Arthur fell into step with them, mopping his brow, where the sweat still lay though the wind was chilly.

"I'll go and have a drink," he said. "The pubs must be open now. Feel I need it."

"Why should you think anyone was aiming at you?" Rose asked, much puzzled. "Why should anyone aim at either of you?"

"Well, I was the one who nearly caught it first. Oh, I suppose it may have been some darned fool after a rabbit. Unnerved me, that's all. Not as brave as I thought! I hope your arm will be all right," he added to Elvan, then nodded and turned away to the Ship Inn.

"I don't understand it at all," said Laura, as they walked on toward the doctor's house in Church Lane. "Oh, you don't know anything, Rose. You laughed at me, but there *is* a mystery. And Elvan and I are trying to find out more." But, before she had gone very far with the story, they reached the doctor's and found him just returning for an early lunch. He whisked Elvan off to his surgery and the two girls sat in the deserted waiting room, while Laura continued to talk. Rose listened incredulously.

"And Elvan believes all that? Thinks the Poldern cups may still be here and that someone's after them?"

"Well, he seems to believe it. So we're curious about all the strangers—the young ones, because my Cockney-Australian voice might belong to one of them, and Mr. Summer, and even Arthur. For Arthur's a stranger, too, and no one really likes him very much. If there *is* anything fishy about him he might have a reason for wanting Elvan out of the way. But he was there and was shot at first. It doesn't make sense."

"In that case, you might be in danger, too. But how would anyone know you're on to the mystery?"

Laura shook her head.

"I don't know. Well, Mr. Summer comes under suspicion there, because I was silly enough to tell him I thought someone was interested in towers. That was before I knew the cups might be involved."

"Mr. Summer was at the back of the crowd," Rose said, looking more alert than she had done for some days. "He came after we did and could have been up there on the cliff paths. He'd get downhill quite quickly, I suppose, even at his age, and it must have taken them some time to decide that it was safe to bring the boat in."

"But Arthur certainly seemed to believe he was the target. He looked really rattled. I thought how terribly white he was when he looked back just before he went into the Ship."

"Some of the strangers were going in after him," Rose remarked. "I'd suspect them first—"

"Yes, I saw Orange Sweater and the dirty one with the beard. Perhaps they needed drinks, too. That kind don't usually carry guns, do they? It's more and more mysterious," said Laura, frowning. "I do hope Elvan's all right."

"You like Elvan, don't you?" Rose asked.

"Yes, of course." Laura was annoyed to feel herself blushing. She wished she could outgrow the awful habit.

"I thought you would. I was sure you'd get on."

"He's very nice, but you needn't think—" Laura began defensively.

Rose stared at her. Perhaps her own experience had given her extra perception.

"Oh, Laura! You haven't. . . . He hasn't. . . . I'd like nothing better!"

"Oh, don't be silly! There's someone else. You said so. And I'll go away, of course, and—"

"There have been plenty of girls. But Mother says she thinks that special one has gone away, to work abroad or something. Anyhow, Elvan hasn't mentioned her for quite a while, and Mother heard through a friend of hers that the girl was restless and talking of traveling."

It was Laura's turn to stare blankly. She was uncomfortably aware that the sudden surge of hope and joy must be all too clear to Rose, but at that moment Elvan came back. There was a neat bandage on his upper arm.

"It's just a graze and nothing to worry about," he said. "Impossible, of course, to tell what kind of bullet it was. Dr. Sims is also convinced it must have been some idiot shooting at rabbits, and aiming out into the river across the cliff. And really, you know, it probably was. I'm no expert at sounds of gunshot. In fact, I scarcely heard the first report, as a seagull was screaming overhead."

"But a few inches difference—" Rose said, as they walked out into Church Lane. "Laura has told me all that's happened."

"Our great mystery!" her brother said lightly, but he was frowning. "It's given me an appetite, anyway, so let's get home to lunch. The thing that puzzles me," he went on, "is Arthur's conviction that *he* was the intended victim. If he can even think that, it seems to mean he knows he has an enemy. And he isn't supposed to have known anyone here until he came. Tell Peter the tale, if you like, Rose, but ask him not to tell his father yet. We may be wildly wrong and the cups can have been in America for twenty years. But Peter will be able to help to keep an eye on things tomorrow. 'May Day will be the best time,' Laura's mysterious voice said. So we'll watch Mr. Summer, and Arthur, and look out for any more suspicious behavior. We still have to find Laura's Cockney-Australian voice. Sure it couldn't have been Arthur, Laura?"

"Yes, I'm sure."

"I don't like any of it," Rose said. "I think you and

Laura are probably mad, but if there's any truth in it you shouldn't keep it to yourselves. You should tell the police and leave it to them."

"Tell Bert Trelawney?" her brother mocked.

"Oh, well, Bert. . . . No, but you could go into Bodmin and ask to see someone."

"And what could we tell? Laura heard voices. I thought someone was following me on a dark road, and someone took potshots at Arthur and me from the cliff. Of course there were the intruders in the towers, but it isn't enough."

"But you do believe there's something?"

Elvan and Laura exchanged glances. At the hint of complicity her heart warmed, but there was fear, too; for say there really was some positive danger? Elvan could have died in the boat that morning.

"I don't know what I believe," Elvan said brusquely. "But tomorrow you girls are to enjoy yourselves. Follow the hoss and keep in the crowd. The most I'll say is that I'm not quite easy about either of you being involved."

"We ought really to watch the towers," Laura said. "It's the towers they're interested in, apparently."

"According to what you heard. Well, we'll see. Actually, the Polderns probably won't leave the Place. The hoss goes up there in the afternoon."

"Peter and I are going to gather boughs," Rose announced, just as they reached the castle.

Elvan laughed.

"Do you want to gather green boughs with me, Laura? You'd have to get up at six and you won't get to bed until after one o'clock. To decorate the town, you know. And primroses and bluebells for the base of the maypole in the square."

"Oh!" cried Laura, who had not heard of this before. "Yes, please!"

"A-maying. Once it would have been hawthorn, I suppose, but since the calendar was changed in the eighteenth century, the hawthorn has flowered too late."

So she would go gathering green boughs with Elvan on May morning! Laura thought during lunch, when the furor caused by Elvan's adventure had died down a little. Even though his father, mother, and Bess believed it must have been some fool shooting at rabbits, it caused sensation enough.

"You girls had better have a couple of hours rest this afternoon," said Mrs. Tregarth, as they rose from the table. "I can see you won't get much sleep tonight."

"I'm going to have tea up at the Place," Rose protested.

"You can still lie down until three-thirty."

Laura went up to her room to rest. But, though she lay on her bed and tried to sleep, her thoughts raced hither and thither. The mystery. . . . May Day. . . . Elvan. Elvan possibly not, after all, nearly engaged to the girl he had known at work.

Once she got up to stand at the window and gaze down at Trepoldern. The afternoon had turned grey and still, and everywhere was very silent. Once more she thought of the hoss, waiting in the loft behind the

The Night Song   127

inn, and she told herself that May Day alone would have been enough. But down in the quiet little port were those two who had whispered on the shore. Two people, she truly believed, were seeking the Poldern cups, and for a moment her mind tried to reconstruct the castle that had once stood where the Tregarths' house now was. The castle had been lived in; the cups had belonged to that lost age, had been fashioned by long-forgotten craftsmen. She didn't really believe that she would ever see the Poldern treasure, yet it could be somewhere in the area.

The day dragged a little. Rose went off to Poldern Place and Laura had tea with the family. Elvan was there, but not talkative. Isaac was there at the start of the meal, but Lelant, who had to come from Bodmin, arrived when they had almost finished. She ate ravenously and said, between bites:

"Isaac and I want to go and sing the 'Night Song' and gather green boughs."

"Not this year, Lellie. You're both too young."

"It isn't fair! It's awful being young," Lelant grumbled.

"It's a state that doesn't last long," said her mother. "You'll have excitement enough on May Day."

The two young ones looked mutinous.

"You underestimate us," Lelant muttered, but Mrs. Tregarth just laughed.

Soon after tea Rose telephoned and asked Laura and Elvan to meet her in the town. Peter would come, too, she said.

They met by the harbor and walked out to the very end of the South Quay. Peter had heard the story from Rose and seemed inclined to be cynical and disbelieving. But it was clear that he respected Elvan enough to go along with him.

"Oh, all right. We'll keep our eyes and ears open tomorrow," he agreed. "If anything is hidden anywhere I should think it must be in the church tower. The thief must have gone rushing down into the town. That Mr. Summer. . . . Yes, I've seen him. Terrible old man, but he *is* old. You can't really believe he's after the cups? And as for Arthur Pengwern, I think he's the *end,* but no possible suspicion can fall on his father. He wasn't even here then."

"No, but—" Then Elvan bit back whatever he had been going to say. He went on instead: "He or Mr. Summer *could* have been one of the whisperers on the shore, but we still have to find Laura's Cockney-Australian voice."

Laura had the feeling that Peter didn't set much store by her "voices." She didn't really blame him. In a strange way Trepoldern was growing more unreal with every hour that passed. It brooded in the grey silence. Impossible to imagine the town decked with green boughs and flowers, the quiet inhabitants released into singing and dancing.

In her room, tidying herself before dinner, Laura stood again at the window. And suddenly music came up to her on the evening air. The beat of a drum, young voices singing a snatch of song; quickly silenced. But

The Night Song   129

those few notes were enough to make her catch her breath. The "May Song?"

Dinner was later than usual that evening, but the children didn't appear until the meal was half over. They arrived giggling and whispering; Mrs. Tregarth reproved them once or twice, and sent them to bed as soon as she could.

"I don't like the pair of you in such tiresome moods. Go and get a good sleep. You'll have a long day tomorrow."

At ten o'clock Mrs. Tregarth said she was going to bed. The night ceremony was short and she wouldn't go to the Great Horse Inn. Bess and Joseph wouldn't go, either. May Day would be enough for them.

At eleven o'clock George Tregarth, Elvan, Rose and Laura drove down into the town. Rose held her father's drum on her knee. The night was still, cold and cloudy, but occasionally the moon rode clear. The streets were ill-lit, but there were people everywhere. The strangers mingled with the inhabitants and ignored the unwelcoming glances.

George Tregarth parked the car just off the square and joined someone he knew. Laura, Rose and Elvan strolled up the narrow street toward the Great Horse Inn, and were joined by Peter Poldern, who appeared from the shadows. Already a crowd was gathered in front of the inn, well wrapped up against the chill night wind. The street was so narrow that people were pressed solidly against the little houses and shops, with their overhanging top stories.

There was a feeling of excited anticipation and everyone seemed in good spirits. The lilting Cornish voices rang in Laura's ears. It seemed very strange to be there, and in some ways she felt an outsider. She stole a glance at Elvan's face, as he laughed and talked with a Trepoldern man. Elvan, still talking, suddenly took her cold hand and tucked it through his arm, the uninjured one. The crowd pressed closer and she began to feel warm.

Suddenly there was a disturbance on the edge of the crowd and some protests. Arthur came elbowing his way through, apologizing breezily. Laura looked at him with dislike. His presence had broken the spell.

"There you all are!" Arthur cried. "I'm sure my name will be mud if my grandparents find out I've come. I expect to find the door bolted against me."

"Well, you couldn't miss it," Elvan said mildly.

"Didn't mean to. I don't get it at all, but I suppose I'll learn."

In the dim light his face looked very different from the way it had appeared that morning. He looked cheerful, even elated. In fact, he emanated a feeling of such powerful excitement that Laura was startled and uneasy. Not because of the night ceremony, surely? She wished him anywhere but at their side. If he was going to talk all the time. . . .

But people were shushing him. Peter Poldern said, "You're ruining the atmosphere!" and Arthur looked offended.

"Not popular, am I?"

A few minutes later he slid away through the crowd and Laura was glad to see him go. All that mattered just now was the magic of the night ceremony.

It was eleven-thirty . . . a quarter to twelve. Suddenly lights came on in front of the Great Horse Inn, showing up the painting of the horse. An upper window opened and a woman looked out. The crowd laughed and shouted greetings, then an almost complete silence fell. And through the quiet crowd that somehow parted to make way for them came several men with drums and accordians. George Tregarth was among them.

Five minutes to twelve. Two minutes to . . . and then, as the clock on the church began to strike, the night came alive. Alive with a strange old tune, with a violent burst of music and song that for a few moments left Laura blinking and dazed, sure that it was after all a complete dream.

"Sing, sing for summer now is come,
The clock strikes twelve and soon 'twill be day-O;
Rejoice, good people, one and all,
Off to the fields and gather the may-O!
Call them all out, knock on the doors,
Old Uncle Ben Trepol as well-O;
Dawn soon will come, flowers they will bloom,
Off we will go to the dell-O!"

The music excited Laura as nothing ever had before. The tune seemed to get into her very bones, and she found herself grasping the words and starting to sing. Led by the musicians, the crowd surged off down the

Led by the musicians, the crowd surged off down the street, pausing here and there before a cottage, calling out those inhabitants who were not already there and singing.

"Sing, sing for summer now is come—"

It was hard to believe. It was dark and cold. But oh, it was wonderful! Wonderful! Laura felt part of the long centuries, for the first time reaching back into an unimaginable past, the ancient past of England.

Elvan kept hold of her as they moved along in the crowd. Everyone had dropped into a lilting, rhythmic walk, their bodies moving in unison. Not far away she saw Rose and Peter, both singing lustily. Rose's face was happy and alive. Fat old women and bald old men were singing. Even the strangers seemed to have merged with the crowd. She saw several of them, singing, too. Mr. Summer, his hair more straggly than ever, had his mouth wide open. He looked peculiar, but not villainous, Laura thought.

The crowd surged along another narrow street and came back to the Great Horse Inn. For the last time the Night Song rang out, then the drums and accordions were silent, the lights on the inn went out. And in the sudden silence a voice said from somewhere at the back of the crowd:

"So what happens now? Do they all go off to the woods in the dark?"

And Laura recognized the voice. It was unmistakably the one she had heard down on the shore, the Cockney-Australian voice that had spoken of the Poldern Cups!

and danger. Elvan felt her jump and glanced down at her, though the street was now so dark he could hardly see her face.

"What is it?" he murmured.

"That voice! It was the one I heard. Elvan, we must find out who it is!"

But the lingering crowd and the darkness beat them. There was no way of knowing who had spoken.

12. The Poldern Folly

"But you did hear it, too?" Laura asked. She was shivering, partly with cold and partly with nervous excitement.

"I heard it," Elvan agreed. "And I think it was probably an Australian accent, not Cockney. An unpleasant voice, at all events. I shouldn't think its owner is a very nice character. A pity we couldn't find him."

The crowd had almost dispersed and the town now seemed vaguely sinister in its darkness and coldness. Rose and Peter came up quickly.

"Father's waiting for us," said Rose. "The lights have gone out in the square. It's all over for a few hours. What's the matter?"

They explained, as they all walked toward the square. Peter made no comment; perhaps he was not even listening.

"Well, we're no better off if you couldn't find him," Rose said. She yawned and shivered, drawing her coat collar up around her chin. "Brrr! It's more like winter than the beginning of summer!"

"Still want to come a-gathering?" Peter asked, and she said yes, she did, and she'd meet him on the road to the Place about six-thirty.

"The only woods hereabouts are at the back of the Place," Peter explained to Laura. "And there's our lime avenue to the house, of course. Those leaves are always out early. Father's always allowed people to cut as many boughs as they want. See you all in the morning, then." And he strode away into the darkness.

The drive to the castle was quickly over, and they were glad to find flasks of coffee and plates of sandwiches awaiting them on the living room table. Fifteen minutes later they were on their way to bed.

In spite of all the excitement Laura fell asleep at once, and was awakened by Bess when it was only just starting to grow light.

"It's going to be a grand day, me dear. Here's some tea and toast. The others are awake."

May morning! Laura leaped out of bed and gazed out at the grey and silver scene. The events of the previous night were still vivid in her mind, and more was to come. Her scalp prickled at the thought of the Great Horse. Even the mystery seemed unimportant when she was soon going to walk through the spring woods with Elvan.

She put on plenty of warm clothes and joined the others in the hall. Rose was yawning and sleepy-eyed, but Elvan seemed as alert as if he had had eight hours sleep. They went out into the cold, clear morning, where there was still no color. Only a sky turning to brighter silver, faintly shining water, and the town and cliffs greyish.

They took Elvan's car and were soon passing through the town and taking the narrow road that led uphill to Poldern Place. There were plenty of young people abroad, all making their way, mostly in pairs, toward the woods. Where there was space to park they met Peter, and, all armed with knives and thin rope, they took a broad track that disappeared among the trees.

The sun came up almost at that moment and there was a burst of birdsong. Laughter sounded here and there and the air smelled fresh and earthy. Many of the trees were still only in bud, but there were chestnuts and sycamores on the edge of the wood and the limes close to the house. They worked at first in a group of four, carrying branches back to the car; not dragging them for fear of spoiling the delicate growth.

"Now primroses and bluebells," said Peter, and they wandered into the heart of the wood. Rose and Peter went off together, and Laura, picking steadily, was happy and at peace. The enchanting morning seemed almost too good to be true and for once she did not find the loveliness of spring vaguely saddening. The place and the person. . . . Well, she had both.

They had worked around until they were well behind the house, in the depths of the wood. There was still a good path, and primroses grew thickly on the banks. There were still voices in the distance, but she and Elvan seemed very much alone in their part of the wood.

Elvan was still cutting the occasional leafy bough, and Laura was ahead. Suddenly she straightened her back and looked directly in front of her and her heart gave a violent leap. For a moment she could hardly believe her eyes. For not far away, bowered in trees and close-growing bushes, was a grey tower. Well, a kind of tower—a very ornate and peculiar-looking building. The tower part had stone carvings and some Gothic pinnacles, but the lower story was quite large, squarish, with boarded-up windows.

Laura stared and gasped, and Elvan joined her quickly.

"It's the Poldern Folly," he explained. "Do you know, I never gave it a thought, and presumably Rose and Peter didn't, either. I don't think they have their minds on our mystery."

"But it *is* a tower! Is it always called the Folly?"

"Sometimes John Poldern's Folly. Though I have heard the local people call it John's Tower. Well, that was daft of me, but I haven't been so far into these woods for years. Oh, it dates from 1890 or thereabouts. John Poldern was squire then, and a pretty odd character, by all accounts. A bit of a recluse. He had this place built and sometimes stayed here alone for days, leaving his wife and children in possession of the house. The local people don't seem to like it much. There's a story that it's haunted."

"So if the thief was a local man would he have come here in the dark to hide the cups?" Laura murmured. She walked very slowly forward.

138   The May Day Mystery

"I don't know," said Elvan, frowning. "He must have been pretty desperate, remember. He could have got back to the town quite easily if he'd wanted to. The path goes on behind the Folly and joins a narrow road. There's quite a tangle of lanes. One way to Trepoldern; then it joins the lane that leads to the cove at the mouth of the river. A third lane doubles back to the Bodmin road after about half a mile. He wouldn't have been stuck."

"But is there anywhere to hide anything in this place? You must have known it as a child."

Elvan grinned. "We were Cornish kids, born and bred. Peter quite believed his ancestor haunted the place. It's even eerier in high summer when the trees are thick."

"It's eerie now," Laura whispered. But she still went forward, her cold hands filled with primroses.

"Peter's father rather liked it once. When he was a young man he used to study here during his university vacations. I remember he laughed at us when we were around seven or eight. He kept the place in order at one time, but it looks pretty derelict now."

The birdsong seemed to have died and no voices sounded in the wood. The sunlight still shimmered on the awakening boughs, but the tower seemed very dark. It had a kind of terrace with broken urns, and there was a grotesque carving over the door. The door itself was open and Laura drew back. Elvan stepped past her and bent to examine a hanging padlock. It had been wrenched apart.

"Someone broke in," he said.

"Searching the tower," Laura suggested. She was still whispering.

"Well, maybe. Or a tramp wanting a bed. It need not have been done all that recently. Want to look inside?"

Laura nodded, refusing to admit that she was scared. Elvan took out matches and struck one as he led the way. But the small flame was hardly necessary. Some light came in through the door and the boarding over the windows fitted imperfectly. She could just see the big room: dusty, damp and depressing. There were a few pieces of old furniture, almost falling apart. A big wooden chair, with a carved back and armrests; a table covered with mould; something that had once been a sofa, but the padding had been eaten away by mice. On the floor there were some mildewed sacks, some rope and other rubbish.

The walls were of stone blocks, with pillars covered with ugly carving let into the corners. No wonder people expected to see old John's ghost, Laura thought. It was a horrible place.

"Ugh!" she said. "How nasty! But while we're here we may as well take a proper look. Is that a doorway over in that dark corner?"

"Yes, it leads to the tower," said Elvan. He hesitated, looking at her in the dim light. "Perhaps we'd better not. I don't suppose there's anything to see, but I don't think you—"

Laura had a streak of obstinacy, and she didn't think she would ever have the courage to come back alone.

If she was going to look it might as well be with a strong companion.

"Let's just see what's up above," she suggested. And she went first toward the dark corner.

Elvan firmly passed her and, using a match again, announced that the door was open.

"You stay here, Laura. *I'll* take a look. We mustn't be long, because they'll want the boughs and flowers down in the town."

He began to climb. Laura, standing at the bottom, had grown used to the dim light. It was not a real spiral staircase, but something squarer and much easier. The steps were broad and in good repair, though green with damp.

Elvan turned a corner and disappeared. She heard the continuing sound of his footsteps, then there was a startled exclamation. A voice floated down to her—a familiar, fussy voice.

"Oh, I'm so sorry if I startled you, my dear Mr. Tregarth! I heard voices below and thought it must be some of the village lads and lasses. I heard some in the wood just now. So odd of everyone to be up so early. Really most strange."

"They're gathering green boughs," explained Elvan. He still had a sheaf of slender branches over his own shoulder.

"Now, how interesting! Still following the old customs, eh? That is something no one explained to me."

Footsteps were coming down. Laura, who was still

breathing heavily after her fright, leaned against the damp wall and waited. Mr. Summer! Mr. Summer in another tower, and so early in the morning, when he might have thought discovery unlikely. What if he pushed Elvan from behind? Attacked him and then her?

But Elvan appeared quite safely. His face was perhaps a little paler than usual, and his eyes were almost black. He gave Laura a kind of grimace, signaling her to silence.

Mr. Summer came after him, stumbling a little. He seemed to have hurt his foot.

"So careless!" he cried, as he gained the room. "Good morning, my dear. How very charming. . . . Girl with primroses! There was a hole in the floor of the room up there and I was silly enough to twist my ankle. I was resting, waiting for the pain to go off."

"I hope it's nothing much, sir," Elvan said, with an apparent effort.

"It will improve. I shall get back to breakfast, perhaps a little slowly. I'm always an early bird, am I not? And I was so excited by the night ceremony that I was unable to sleep."

"How did you come to find the tower?" Elvan asked, while Laura turned toward the door that led into the open air, into the sweet spring woods that were such a contrast to John Poldern's Folly.

"The landlord at the Ship happened to mention it last night. Otherwise I should not have known of its existence. Quite a monstrosity, but interesting of its period.

These follies. . . . Human beings sometimes get strange notions."

"Someone broke in," Elvan said, casually indicating the broken padlock.

"So I observed. I assure you it was not I. But, since the place was open, I was curious enough to take a look. Now don't let me keep you young people."

"I have the car on the road near the gates of the Place," Elvan said politely. "It's rather full of branches, but I think we could squeeze you in."

"How kind, but I can manage on my own. May morning is a time for romance, and no one wants an old codger like me."

Romance! Well, it had seemed so until Laura saw the Folly. But much of the magic had fled. She was relieved, nonetheless, when Elvan took Mr. Summer at his word. He and Laura hurried ahead, and, as soon as they were out of earshot, Laura said:

"He *must* be one of them. He *was* searching, he must have been. Perhaps he really didn't know about the fifth tower until last night."

Elvan grunted and nodded. He didn't seem to want to talk.

When they reached the car there was a small piece of paper tucked into the windscreen. The note said: "We have taken some of the boughs down into the town. Don't bother about us. Peter and Rose."

"Laura, you've *got* to keep out of it," Elvan told her, as he drove down the hill. "Forget it for today. I'll stick to Mr. Summer like glue."

"But it will spoil May Day!" Laura protested.

"No, it won't. Once the hoss comes out you'll be so thrilled you won't worry about anything. I'll get hold of Peter after breakfast and tell him what's happened. It could be that the old chap was telling the simple truth, but I suspect not. There's probably more to him than meets the eye."

"But—"

They were down in the square. It was eight o'clock and the little shops and cottages were already hung with fresh green. The maypole in the center of the square was also festooned, and near the top, decorated hoops floated out against the blue sky.

"They'd like that lot up at the Great Horse Inn, me dears," said an old man. "Leave the primroses here, please," he added to Laura. He was busy banking flowers around the base of the pole.

Elvan drove up the narrow street and began to pile the boughs against the inn wall. Billy Bailey was already at work with string and nails, and the ancient door was arched with sharply green lime leaves.

"Breakfast now!" said Elvan and turned the car for home. It was clear he wasn't going to discuss the mystery any more and Laura gave in. But how *could* she just think of the hoss when so much might be going on in Trepoldern? Elvan wanted to keep her out of danger, that was clear, and she seemed to have no choice but to obey him.

In a way she was scared enough to be relieved, yet there was also a feeling of rebellion. During that long festive day Elvan couldn't stop her from using her eyes and ears!

She gazed back at the town as they climbed the hill and saw it still quiet and dreaming. But soon it would resound again to that ancient tune.

13. The Mystery of the Great Horse

Everyone else talked so much at breakfast that the comparative silence of Elvan and Laura passed unnoticed. The children were wildly excited, and Rose was exceedingly animated. She still had a faintly feverish air and Laura wondered how long she would continue to feel any kind of happiness. If she herself was aware that time was passing and that they would have to return to London a week on Saturday, Rose must be even more conscious of the fact. And if she had to go back to the house near the Fulham Road with nothing resolved. . . .

Rose—Mr. Summer—that whole extraordinary early morning experience—Laura certainly had plenty to occupy her mind.

The sun was shining brilliantly and the weather man on the radio had spoken of an unseasonably warm day in the southwest. Lelant wore a pink dress, and Isaac white trousers and a white shirt, with a broad green ribbon tied around his waist. He was a miniature of his father, who was attired the same way, except that *his* green band was looped over one shoulder like a baldrick.

"All the men and boys wear white," Mrs. Tregarth explained. "What a blessing it's such a perfect morning!"

After breakfast Elvan disappeared to change, and Laura also went to her room. There would be no need for warm woolens, and she put on a pale yellow dress and a green cardigan. The cardigan was only thin, made of some silky, woven material. How lucky that she could wear the horse's color on May Day!

Her view of Trepoldern was now vividly blue and green, with touches of russet where there was lichen on the old roofs. Most of the boats seemed to be in port and there was not much activity on the quays. Snatches of the May Song accompanied by the heartstopping beating of drums came up to her as she stood at the open window. It was true that the tune cast an extraordinary spell. The music came nearer and a band of children surged into the courtyard—all boys, all in white, all with little drums.

"Sing, sing for summer now is come,
Green grow the leaves and white is the may-O;
Dance, one and all, follow the hoss,
Rejoice on the morning of May-O!"

They circled the courtyard and departed again. Their young voices came floating back as they went down the road.

Laura found that there were tears in her eyes. "Rejoice on the morning of May-O!" Already the atmosphere of the Festival wrapped her around, and perhaps the mystery really didn't matter very much. What mattered most was that the Great Horse would come out at ten-thirty.

They all walked down into the town; everyone, including Bess and Joseph. Joseph was in white, with a green ribbon, and his old face was alight with pleasure.

"I seen seventy-five May Days, me dear," he said to Laura. "My mother told me I screamed at the hoss. Screamed me head off. I was eleven months old at the time. The kids is always a little scared at first. Then they get to know him and realize that he brings good luck."

It was ten o'clock as they reached the square. The leaves were still fresh and green, the base of the maypole bloomed with primroses, bluebells and a few delicate wood anemones. The leaves and floating hoops at the top of the pole looked wonderful against a sky that was now darkly blue.

Everyone was out—locals, the unkempt strangers, and a few ordinary visiting holiday-makers. The town was awake and aware, everyone united in excitement at the imminent appearance of the Great Horse. The children with the drums were still marching, still singing. The leader had a collecting box and was shaking it under the visitors' noses.

The party from the castle soon broke up. Elvan had managed to have a word with Rose and it was he who bore off Peter when he appeared. Laura and Rose stayed together as they pushed their way up the street toward the Great Horse Inn.

"The Folly!" said Rose. "I never thought of that, nor did Peter. They do call it John's Tower. But there still isn't much evidence—"

"There's Mr. Summer!" whispered Laura.

Mr. Summer, still wearing his awful old raincoat, was leaning against a shop opposite the Great Horse Inn.

"And there's Arthur," said Rose.

Arthur had turned out in white along with the inhabitants of Trepoldern. He came up to them, grinning. He explained that the trousers and the green sash had belonged to his father.

"Hidden away in the Vicarage. They're not a bad fit, are they? Hannah told me. She's a miserable old thing, but she quite likes me, and she's keen on the Festival. I wouldn't be surprised if we see her dancing later." He guffawed at the thought.

Laura hoped that they weren't going to have his company when the Great Horse came out. But luckily he drifted away quite soon.

Laura and Rose managed to get a place close to the door of the Great Horse Inn. Rose explained that there was a back entrance to the inn courtyard, but that the horse would make its first appearance through the front door. It always did, though the entrance was narrow.

"Do you know, I'm quite scared," Laura confessed.

Rose laughed.

"So am I. I've seen it since I was a baby, but it still means something . . . something one can't explain. The hoss gets a life of its own."

"How many, many years people must have waited here!"

"The inn was built in 1604, and there are records to prove the hoss was kept here from the beginning. But that's quite modern, as the Festival goes. It started centuries and centuries before Christ, when England was ... Well, what was it then? People believed in old gods."

Did they still? Laura wondered, as the minutes ticked away. Was it now just a jolly thing, an excuse for singing and dancing and collecting money for charity?

She turned and saw Elvan and Peter not far away. Even after only a few days in Trepoldern she could recognize many faces in the tightly packed crowd, even among the strangers. There was Orange Sweater and the one with the beard. One girl actually had a small baby strapped to her shoulders. An odd lot, the strangers, and someone with dangerous business in Trepoldern might be hiding among them. But they were quiet now; not causing any trouble. They stood as silently as the local people, waiting for the hoss.

It was twenty-five past ten. Laura's heart seemed to miss a beat. She kept her eyes on the dark entrance to the inn. There was a short passage, then the courtyard. She could glimpse it occasionally when people moved.

The narrow street was still mainly in shadow. Flags moved gently overhead in the faint, warm breeze. It was extraordinarily silent; a breathless, expectant hush. Quietly the men with drums and accordions came through the crowd, which somehow parted to let them through. Some of the musicians were old; they had seen many May Days. They grouped themselves to one side of the door.

The seconds and minutes ticked away. The hush was complete, almost awesome. On the edge of the crowd, a baby gave a cry, quickly hushed. Trepoldern waited for the appearance of the Great Horse.

And then, with a stabbing terror and surprise that was totally inexplicable, the hoss was there! It burst through the dark entrance, the great frame on one side to take the narrow lintels. A great black form, with a tiny horse's head at the front and the grotesque mask in the middle. A black and shining thing, old as time.

The crowd drew in a concerted breath, and the music struck up with a burst of sound that was almost terrible.

"Sing, sing, for summer now is come. . . ."

The horse surged down the street in the wake of the musicians, tossing violently, seeming almost to reach from house front to house front. The crowd fell in behind; singing, moving as one to the compelling rhythm.

Then, so suddenly that Laura who was near the front almost fell on the shining tarpaulin that was the horse, the creature sank down on to the cobblestones of the old street. The tune changed, growing sad and even more ancient.

"Oh, why is he dead? Oh, why did he die?
Old Uncle Ben Trepol as well-O;
The gulls they do cry and fall from the sky,
And loud tolls the bell-O."

Many of the inhabitants of Trepoldern actually went down with the hoss. It was the death of the earth in winter. The strange little head lay on the ground and the teaser bent over it, waving his green and white stick. The teaser was a very old man, who must have seen eighty May Days at least.

The horse was dead. . . . Would he ever live again? But "Live! Live!" shouted the crowd, and the hoss was up again, dancing along the street, with the teaser going backward in front of it. The tune was triumphant. Summer was born. . . . the earth would live again. . . . the corn would grow high.

"Sing, sing, for he lives again,
  Green grow the leaves and white is the May-O;
  Dance, one and all, follow the hoss,
  And luck be with you in May-O!"

Laura had forgotten everything but the Great Horse. She followed in a trance, so close to the tossing frame that occasionally she had to put up her hand to save herself from injury. It was clear that it was immensely heavy. When the hoss surged forward, tossing from side to side, the crowd drew back, pressing against the house and shop fronts.

In the square the dying ceremony was repeated, as it would be repeated a hundred, or even hundreds of times throughout the long day. The teaser's baton changed hands. Laura saw that it was Bess facing the hoss. The old woman's arms had gone up into a strange position; she was doing a kind of dance that seemed familiar to everyone else. When the hoss died she crouched down, her gaze intent. She had certainly forgotten her rheumatism. In her whole life Laura had never seen anything stranger; she was lost, not thinking of Elvan or the mystery.

"Sing, sing, for he lives again—"

And so it went on. Up and down every narrow street, along the harbor. The music never stopping, the hoss going on its gleaming black way, the pointed mask brilliant green, black and white in the sun.

Yet the men did take turns. Laura saw, on more than one occasion, someone crawl out from under the frame and someone else take his place. It made no difference. The hoss had its own life, one day in the year for unimaginable ages.

On the North Quay the hoss chased Orange Sweater, leaping and tossing and moving at a fast pace. It was a grotesque sight; the shining black thing with the prehistoric mask and Orange Sweater running and dodging, plain terror on his face. Those of his friends who were near laughed, apparently looking forward to seeing him get a ducking. But, just in time, the sweating young man managed to pass the hoss and run back to where there was less danger of a sudden swim.

Laura followed everywhere. Sometimes Rose was with her, but they often got separated. She was still in a trance, but she noticed some things that seemed curious. Lelant and Isaac, whenever she saw them, seemed to be with Arthur; and that was odd, as they didn't like him. Once she was near enough to see him scowl and hear him say: "Where are all your friends? Don't you want to join them?" And Lelant smiled sweetly and said something in reply that wasn't audible to Laura.

The Mystery of the Great Horse   153

She noticed that the bearded young man seemed always somewhere near Arthur and once she saw them exchange a few words. And she also was aware that Mr. Summer, limping slightly, seemed determined not to miss any of the festivities. In spite of his peculiar appearance he looked alert, his gaze darting everywhere.

Of Elvan and Peter there was no sign since she had glimpsed them in the crowd a few minutes after the horse reached the square. And it was after twelve o'-clock when she saw them again. Then Peter captured Rose and Elvan took Laura by the arm and drew her into a quiet street. The hoss was still down by the harbor.

"What have you been doing?" Laura asked.

"Oh, we took the opportunity of looking at the church tower, but there's no sign of a hiding place of any kind and no one came. Except the Vicar, who met us just leaving the church and seemed surprised. Then we went up to the Folly and had a good look around there. Peter says he knows of no hiding place, and I think he's still skeptical. We did take a look at the hoss in between, and Arthur and Mr. Summer always seemed to be there."

"Yes, they were," Laura agreed. "And, it's strange, but Lellie and Isaac won't leave Arthur alone."

"Got a crush on him!" their brother said lightly.

"I shouldn't think so. They don't like him. Oh, Elvan, I think the Festival is wonderful! I—I'm finding it quite hard to think of anything but the Great Horse."

"That's a good girl," he said, amused. "I thought it

would get you. The hoss will be going in for about an hour and a half soon, so we'll go back to lunch. I don't think anything untoward will happen, after all."

"The day isn't over yet," said Laura.

"No. It goes on until nine-thirty."

Elvan was still with Laura when the hoss danced its way back to the Great Horse Inn and that time entered the courtyard by the back way. Everyone crowded up against the low wall to see the mask taken off to reveal the hot, good-looking face of a young fisherman. He crouched down and came out of the frame, then mask and frame were carefully put away in the loft.

"Billy Bailey starts off again at two," Laura was told.

As they climbed the hill to the castle, snatches of the May Song still came up from the town, where the tireless children were still parading and dancing. The tune filled Laura's head and she knew it would haunt her always. If she went away from Trepoldern and never saw it again, those modal notes would recur in her dreams. Go away from Trepoldern. . . . Oh, so soon! The thought was so awful that she pushed it away.

They were all back at the inn a few minutes before two o'clock. This time there were not so many people waiting, because the women had to clear up after lunch. But the holiday makers and strangers seemed to be there in full force, and so were the three young policemen. They were talking together earnestly, a little apart.

Mr. Summer came bustling along, looking rather distraught. He didn't answer Laura's greeting, and in fact seemed not to see her.

"What's the matter with *him?*" Rose whispered.

"And where's Arthur?" asked Elvan.

"Oh, still having a ghastly lunch at the Vicarage," said Rose, and giggled.

They stood against the wall, for it was only for the ceremonial first appearance that the hoss came out of the front door of the inn. And just as the church clock struck two, the hoss came bursting out of the loft doorway. For a few moments the hidden bearer seemed to find some difficulty, and then the rhythmic tossing began, keeping in time to the music.

"Around the town again first," said Peter. "Then up to the Place and to some of the new houses on the hill. The hoss usually goes to the Place last, then walks back down the hill."

None of the morning's magic had abated and Laura again found herself lost, under a spell. The hoss seemed to be dancing more violently than ever as it surged down the street.

"Old Billy Bailey's got his energy back!" someone cried.

The crowd had thickened and pressed close. It was quite hot in the narrow streets of the town. The hoss died and lived again as it went on its way. Mr. Summer was following, but there was still no sign of Arthur, and the children had disappeared. For a moment Laura felt a little anxious, but really it was difficult to see exactly who was there.

The strangers, however, were still much in evidence, though mostly keeping a respectful distance from the hoss. The bearded young man was there and the hoss seemed to single him out. The young man laughed, but moved quickly, trying to get out of the way. Finally and incongruously, he took to his heels, and there was much laughter from the townspeople as the hoss went in pursuit. But the stranger was unencumbered by a great frame and he was rapidly gaining distance.

For a moment the whole scene was imprinted on Laura's mind. Rose and Peter had been well ahead and had seemed to be paying no attention to the hoss's capers behind them. But they turned at the sound of laughter and watched the unfortunate stranger, who was by then almost level with them.

Suddenly there was a sharp report; the fleeing figure seemed to pause, and swung half-around, so that the crowd saw his startled face. Then he crumpled in a heap on the cobblestones, almost at Rose's feet.

And Rose gave a shrill scream, went deathly white and almost fell into Peter's arms.

"Someone shot him!"

"Yes, he's been shot!"

"And the lassie as well? There was only one shot!"

The music had stopped and the musicians were running. Everyone was running, passing the hoss, which still tossed a little, as though not quite aware that disaster had struck the Festival.

Laura started to run with the rest, tripped on the cobblestones and her shoe came off. She was almost mowed down in the rush as she fished for it and struggled to get it on again. Everyone was gathering around the fallen man and she just glimpsed Rose, certainly not dead, but still with Peter's arm around her.

Laura noticed one other thing as she ran past the horse and pressed herself against the back of the crowd, trying to see. Mr. Summer, who was taller than she had thought, was closest to the fallen man. He was shouting something, almost as if he were giving orders.

The whole thing was a shambles, with people pushing and shouting, struggling in the narrow street. No one was paying attention to anyone else, but only wanting to understand what had happened and causing chaos because of it.

It was hopeless; Laura couldn't see. She drew back, wondering if she could run around another way and get to the front. Turning, she saw the circular, shining black cover of the hoss lying on the cobblestones, with the mask tossed aside and grinning eerily in the gutter.

Billy Bailey must have got out and gone to see what was happening. The thought went through Laura's mind just a fraction of a second before she noticed the small, round hole in the tarpaulin. A hole with a hint of burning around the edges. In the next second she saw what everyone else in Trepoldern missed; a figure just disappearing into the shadows of an alley way.

14. Laura to the Rescue

Arthur Pengwern! Laura was sure it had been he. And somehow, not understanding why, she knew at once that it had not been Billy Bailey under the framework, but Arthur. She knew that he had shot at the fleeing stranger through the horse's trappings. That it was some kind of deathly charade.

She gave one quick glance around, but could not see Elvan anywhere. So, not stopping to reason with herself, she started to run after Arthur. If she tried to attract attention and help she would only lose him. He didn't know she had seen him. She would never have done so if her shoe hadn't come off and she hadn't gotten stuck at the back of the crowd.

A few thoughts did pass through her mind as she ran. What a risk he had taken—he must be utterly foolhardy or mad. Anyway, she had to know where he was going before she raised the alarm; otherwise he'd disappear, hide the gun, and no one would ever be able to prove it.

That end of the street was quite deserted, silent in

the warm May afternoon. The alley way, when she reached it, was empty, too. It was only a narrow cut between cottages and she ran fleetly along it, pausing at the corner to look out into the lane at the back. It was a lane that she recognized. It went up to Poldern Place, and Arthur was just disappearing around a steep corner.

Laura, panting and shaking a little, continued in pursuit. Afterwards plenty of people were to tell her how foolish she had been, but at the time it seemed the only course. Just to keep him in sight . . . know where he hid the gun.

Arthur! The villain of the piece, after all! One of the villains. And had the dirty, hairy young man been the other? As she went up the lane, between the banks bright with primroses, a few words came unbidden into her mind. The whispering voice on the shore had said: "I wouldn't put it past you to doublecross me." And Arthur had been shot at in the boat; he had known he had an enemy. So he had taken that dramatic—that wholly mad—way of killing someone.

Still, he had gotten away with it. No one had suspected that the shot had come from the hoss. All eyes had been on the fleeing victim.

Laura reached the corner and peered cautiously around it. Arthur was fifty yards ahead, only a short distance from the gates of the Place. He was turning into the woods. He must be going to the Folly.

Should she go back now and call for help? Or should she run on to the Place and tell them there? Ask them to telephone the police in Bodmin? But the precious cups were involved, they just must be. She remembered Arthur's changed manner of the night before; his unexplained elation. So he had found them, and was he now going to get them?

He still had no idea she was behind him. Luckily her shoes had rubber soles, and he had never looked back. She was in no danger so long as she went quietly and remained hidden. And what if Mark Poldern wasn't at the Place? They didn't expect the hoss until later and he might well be at one of the farms. If there was no one at the house but Mrs. Poldern and the old servants. . . . They'd never believe her. Mrs. Poldern might refuse to let her telephone the police. Time would be wasted and Arthur might get away with the cups.

Laura turned into the woods, onto the track she and Elvan had followed that morning. Fortunately it wound a good deal, the primrose banks were quite high and there were bushes as well as trees. The only danger was if Arthur changed his mind and came back.

But he showed no sign of turning back. Each time she peered ahead he was just going around the next curve of the path. He was a conspicuous figure in his white clothes, which showed up against the green and brown. She thought there was a bulge in his right-hand trouser pocket and her heart quailed. The gun?

Well, anyway, it was too late to change her own mind. She was committed. But she thought of Elvan with longing. Where had he been during those moments of pursuit and sudden panic? Somewhere in the crowd. They had been together and then separated just

Laura to the Rescue   161

before the hoss chased the stranger.

Well, she would hide in the undergrowth within sight of the tower and just watch. If Arthur came out carrying something, she would follow again. Instinct told her that Arthur must have found the Poldern treasure. Nothing else could explain his actions. The cups—the golden, jeweled cups, beyond price. Had they been in John Poldern's Folly for twenty years?

She crawled the last few yards through grass and bushes and came within sight of the brooding Folly. Arthur was just going through the door. He looked quite easy and casual. Clearly he had no fear of pursuit and discovery.

Laura crept nearer, remembering that the window in the tower was not boarded and that the other boards didn't fit well. She must remain hidden, whatever happened.

But what did happen within the next few seconds was something she had never expected. Young frightened screams rang out, and Arthur's voice followed, harsh and loud:

"What are *you* doing here? I've had just about enough of you both today! Make another sound and I'll shoot you dead."

"*No!*" It was Lelant. "We aren't doing any harm. What are you doing with a gun?"

"You'll soon see. I've no time for arguing. I've made my plans and no one is going to stop me. Certainly not you two kids. . . ."

Laura crouched there, terrified and sick. Lellie and

Isaac. . . . They *had* been behaving oddly. Had they somehow gotten themselves involved in the mystery? Perhaps they had suspected Arthur all along. Seen him at the tower, perhaps, and somehow drawn their own conclusions.

"You'd never dare to shoot us!" That was Isaac, trying to sound brave, breaking into the harangue.

"Oh, wouldn't I? You won't be the first I've killed. Get over there in that corner."

Laura rose to her full height and ran toward the Folly. She fully believed that Arthur was mad, probably now with a lust for killing. And Rose's little brother and sister had already made themselves dear to her. Arthur couldn't shoot *three*. She would tell him—she would tell him. . . .

She shot over the terrace, missed her footing and fell against one of the ancient urns. It fell with a crash, with Laura on top of it. She was up in a moment and turning to face Arthur as he came through the doorway, the gun in his hand.

"You!"

"Yes, me" croaked Laura. A piece of broken stone had cut her leg. She could feel the blood coursing warmly down into her shoe. But it didn't matter. Nothing mattered but convincing Arthur; stopping him from doing any more shooting.

"I heard the children. You can't shoot them. People would hear at the house. It's not so far away through the trees. And they're searching for you . . . people in the town. They'll be this way very soon. I ran ahead."

Arthur looked at her. His eyes certainly looked wild. "You're lying!" he said thickly.

"No, I'm not." Perhaps they really were searching for the killer now.

"Come on in."

Laura obeyed. She couldn't think what else to do. Lellie and Isaac were crouching close together in a corner of the dismal room, their faces white and terrified.

"Oh, Laura!" cried Lelant.

Arthur stood there, swinging the gun. Across his face passed several expressions, none of them pleasant.

"Maybe they would hear at the house. Maybe I'll take you all to somewhere where no one will hear." A pause, then a sudden ghastly lightening of his expression. "No, I know. That will be far better. And a more suitable punishment for meddling folk. Not so quick, but quick enough. I think the tide will be just right."

Laura didn't understand how his mind was working, but clearly he had some cruel plan. She had saved the children once, but now they all seemed in desperate danger.

Arthur waved the gun at her.

"You and the kids go over by the tower door. One slightest movement from any of you and I'll shoot and risk it."

Laura looked at the shivering children, then she took Lelant's hand. It was icy cold.

"Come on, Lellie."

Arthur watched them crossing the room to the darkest corner, some distance from the outer door.

"It can't do you any good to know. I've got the cups and I'm getting clear away with them."

He walked to the opposite corner, to an angle between a window and a carved pillar. He reached up to a level above his head and did something to one of the flat, oblong stones. They all watched him, half-hypnotized.

The whole large stone swung out, and he reached up to grope in the dark cavity thus revealed. Not a singing stone, thought Laura, but a *swinging* one. Old John Poldern had made a hiding place in his Folly. And someone had known twenty years ago. That long-ago thief and murderer must have come through the dark woods and hidden the cups there. But it couldn't have been Arthur himself, or his father.

Arthur's hands had come away holding a bundle. The light was poor, but it looked like a leather bag, not very large. He stood for a moment, gloating down at it.

"Treasure... worth a mint of money. You'd like to see, wouldn't you, but there isn't time. We've got to go."

He glanced around the room and then bent to pick up some of the rope that lay on the floor among the old sacks.

"This will come in useful. Get moving. Keep in front and don't make a sound. We're going around the back of the Folly and over to the other road."

"Laura!" whispered Lelant, her small hand tightly clutching Laura's own.

"We'll have to go," said Laura. She was surprised that

Laura to the Rescue   165

her voice sounded almost normal. "Don't try to do anything silly. He *will* shoot."

"I'm glad you're being so sensible," sneered Arthur. For a moment, as Laura crossed the room with the children their eyes met. "You were too keen on that Elvan by half," Arthur said savagely. "And both of you too nosy. You deserve all that's coming to you. If you'd been nicer to me—"

"It wouldn't have made any difference," said Laura, with a desperate, cold dignity.

Arthur laughed. "Too right!"

They circled the Folly and took the broad, clear path. Laura prayed that there would be someone taking a stroll in the woods, but it seemed unlikely that help would come that way. Everyone was down in Trepoldern, presumably still puzzling over the terrible happening.

The woods were as sweet as they had been that morning, but death walked behind, in the shape of Arthur Poldern.

15. The Rising Tide

Laura felt desperately sorry for the children. They stumbled often on the woodland path, and Lelant was crying quietly.

"Oh, won't someone stop him?" Isaac whispered. "Won't someone come?"

But no one came at all, and quite soon they saw a narrow lane in front of them. Just before the lane, driven into a thicket, stood Arthur's old car.

Arthur unlocked the doors, never taking his eyes off them; then he reached in and drew out an old raincoat. He put it on in one quick movement and then waved the gun again.

"That's better," he said. "I was too conspicuous in these white togs. First opportunity I get I'll change my trousers. Oh, I'm not taking a single chance; I have all my stuff with me." Then he said sharply to the children: "Get into the back. And no monkey tricks. In the front beside me, Laura."

"But—"

"Get in!" His tone was savage. "Or I'll risk shooting

you all here and now and hiding your bodies in the bushes."

As Laura obeyed he went around to the other door and climbed into the driving seat. He dumped the small leather bag on the floor between their feet and placed the gun in the small compartment under the steering wheel.

"Don't try anything," he warned. He started the car and drove off so violently that the bushes crackled and the car almost missed the turning into the lane.

"But where are you taking us?" Laura asked, through stiff lips. He had said something about the tide. Surely he hadn't a boat waiting somewhere along the coast?

"I have an idea," he said, almost with elation. "I'll put you all somewhere where you won't be found until it's far too late. You'll tell no tales, and I shall be away in Plymouth. You mightn't be found for days—no one will think of looking there."

Elvan had said that one branch of the lane led back to the town, but Arthur was not driving that way. What else had Elvan said? A lane that joined the Bodmin road and the way that led to the river mouth.

"You'll never get away with it," said Laura. She was terrified, but there was anger, too. She *had* been a fool, perhaps—but if she hadn't followed Arthur the children would almost certainly be dead by now.

"Oh, I shall," Arthur said airily. "Most of this was planned. I packed my things early this morning and put them in the car. Then I drove it up here and hid it. I've left a note under my pillow, where it will be found eventually, saying that I can't stand the quiet life and am going to London to look for a job. But I'm going to Plymouth, where I have a contact. He'll take the cups and pay me a handsome sum. Not the true value of the cups, of course, but more than enough to give me a start in life. Then I'll change my name and disappear. The car will be sold, or dumped. No one will know where I've gone, or have any real reason for looking for me. They'll think I left long before the shooting."

"They'll put two and two together. Someone was shot and you disappear—"

"Huh!" Arthur swerved violently past a signpost that said "Bodmin" to the left and "Poldern Head" slightly to the right. Laura still looked desperately for any sign of life, for someone on the road or in the fields. There was an abandoned tractor, painted brilliant red, in the middle of the field on the left, but she saw no one.

"You all got on to something, clearly," Arthur said. "But there's no evidence. The only one I'm doubtful about is Elvan Tregarth. Did he tell you he thinks I'm not Arthur Pengwern?"

"No," said Laura, surprised by the question. "He certainly didn't." But Elvan had searched Arthur's room, and found his passport. He had said that it was all right.

"Something happened in the boat that day he had lunch in St. Austell. He saw me without my shirt. I had happened to fall into the water and had taken it off to dry. He tried to cover up what he thought, but I guessed. Something about Arthur Pengwern having a scar for life because he was injured by a shark just before his parents died."

"I never heard about that." Keep him talking, Laura thought, dazed. "We thought there was some mystery, someone looking for the cups, but he tried to keep me out of it."

"But now you're in it up to the neck!" said Arthur, with a guffaw. "He can't have been sure. I passed it off when I found out how his mind was working. He'd heard about it as a kid, in letters from Australia, and been so horrified he'd never forgotten. I said the surgeons did a good job."

"Did they?" croaked Laura.

"I don't know, because I'm not Arthur Pengwern. That startles you, eh? No harm in telling you, because you haven't a hope. I'm like him enough. . . . I have Cornish blood. I got away with it."

"Then—Who are you?"

"That'd be telling. Poor old Arthur is dead, and probably eaten by sharks by this time."

None of it could be true. Laura clutched the side of the car as they hurtled over the rough road toward the river mouth. He was mad as a hatter. She thought of the silent children in the back and wondered what she could do to save them a second time. She didn't think there was any chance of getting the gun. It was much nearer to Arthur and he would foil the slightest movement.

"You probably killed that young man, the hairy one," she said. "Who was he?"

"A menace," said Arthur, laughing in a frightening way. "Wanted to share. As though I would. I never liked him. He was my stepbrother."

"An Australian?"

"Of course. I came as Arthur, and he insisted on coming, too. It was just good luck for him that there were all those odd bods and he fitted in."

"But Mr. Summer?" They were almost at the end of the road. Beyond a brilliant band of gorse, she saw the shining sea. Not far over to their right was the lovely, peaceful path she and Rose had walked on that first morning. Ahead was the cliff edge, empty of cars. Arthur must have counted on that, on everyone being in Trepoldern.

"Him?" Arthur looked blank. "That rum old man? Nothing to do with me. Just a bore. Nutty."

"He didn't look nutty when last I saw him." But there was no time to understand. What did Arthur mean to do with them?

She soon knew.

"I think there'll just be time to get you into the Cave of the Great Horse before the tide comes up," said Arthur.

When she moved a fraction Laura could see the children in the mirror. They sat huddled together, their faces white and scared. They hadn't made a sound all the way.

At the same moment her ankle touched the leather bag Arthur had dumped on the floor and her skin seemed to crawl with awareness. In that bag was the precious treasure; two beautiful things that must not be lost again. If Arthur got away with them to Plymouth they might be out of the country on a ship before anything could be done. Arthur himself might be on a ship, under another identity.

He had stopped the car and was turning it on the short grass of the cliff top, evidently ready for a getaway. Laura gave another frantic look around. There were no small boats on the water, though she could see a ship far away. Someone had to come ... something had to happen. Was he planning to shoot them in the cave?

Arthur fished in his left hand pocket and glanced down at the coil of rope he had put there.

"We'll need this," he said. Then he added: "Out!" and got out himself, the gun in his hand. He shut and locked his door.

The children obeyed quite quickly, leaving the car on Laura's side. Arthur was beside them in two or three strides. Then Isaac did a silly, heroic thing. He charged at Arthur, striking at the gun and butting him in the stomach.

Arthur staggered and gasped, but did not drop the gun. Laura thought fleetingly that it was only luck it had not gone off and killed or maimed Isaac.

"Run!" screamed Isaac, and "Don't!" ordered Laura. For he would only shoot. Still gasping, turned away from her, Arthur was muttering: "You little devil! You wait! I'll—"

In those moments Laura did a silly, heroic thing herself. The front door on her side was still open. She bent

172   The May Day Mystery

and seized the leather bag, which seemed quite light. ... the cups must only be small. She hurled it as far from her as she could into the gorse bushes, which were only a few feet away and growing close and high. The bag went well in and sank with only a faint sound of crackling gorse.

Arthur spun around, eyes watering, face savage.

"What was that?"

"I thought there was someone," said Laura, staring at the bushes. No good looking the other way.

Arthur, enraged and jumpy, seemed not to have full control of his mind. He did not look into the car, but advanced toward the bushes. Laura slammed the door, so that he might not notice the absence of the precious cargo. Arthur immediately rounded on her.

"Only shutting it," she said, astonished that her voice was level, almost casual.

"There's no one there," said Arthur, locking the door Laura had just closed. "Must have been a rabbit or a bird. Get going and let's have no more nonsense. Down the cliff path."

They started off obediently, the children stumbling and Lelant whimpering. The cove below looked beautiful and serene. The rising tide was washing around the black rocks. There was some sand left uncovered, but not very much.

The air was sweet and warm, the sound of the sea was a faint surge and whisper. It seemed incredible that death could be so near on a perfect afternoon.

"Keep ahead," ordered Arthur. "Go into the cave."

The Cave of the Great Horse loomed blackly under the cliff. The children hesitated and were prodded with the gun. Inside it was pretty dark, with a dank sea smell. Laura remembered it well from that first happy morning with Rose, but she had not actually gone in. And now Arthur drove them right to the back of the cave, which turned out not to be large.

"Rings," said Arthur, with satisfaction. His voice echoed. "I found them the other day and didn't know then they'd come in so useful. Each of you stand against one, and one movement by anyone and I'll shoot and risk it. There may be lovers out on the cliff somewhere, but I doubt it."

He tied up Isaac and then Lelant, so that their hands were behind them, secured to a heavy iron ring. Then he advanced on Laura. By then her legs were so weak she could hardly stand. His diabolical plan was all too clear. There was seaweed on ledges above her head. The high tide would gradually drown them—and it wouldn't be very long.

"You *won't* get away with it!" she said. "They'll block the roads and bridges. Cornwall is more cut off than the rest of England. You'll be trapped."

"If it hadn't been for you I'd have been away by now," he said, with that suppressed savagery. "But there's a tangle of lanes. I can go over Bodmin Moor. They won't have got on to it, but I can ditch the car and thumb a lift into Plymouth."

Laura's hands were tied painfully with the last of the rope. He examined all the knots, then snapped shut the knife he had used to cut the rope and put it in his pocket. Turning away to the cave mouth he said:

"Got to go now, or I'll be cut off with you. A pity you didn't stay out of it." Then he had left the cave at a run, turned to the right and disappeared.

They could all see the cove and the rising water. Lelant was crying.

"The spring tides are high," Isaac said, in a muffled voice. "The water will be over our heads in half an hour."

"I know," said Laura. "Oh, why on earth did you get involved? How did you *know?*"

"We didn't exactly know," explained Lelant, through her tears. "We kind of 'deducted.' And we followed Arthur and Mr. Summer when we could. We saw Arthur go to the Folly yesterday evening before dinner. He came out looking.... Well, as if he'd found a fortune. He didn't see us, and when he'd gone we went to search, but couldn't find anything. That stone would have been too high for us, but we didn't know that. So we thought we'd try again this afternoon, and—and he c-caught us."

However it had been, they were facing death and no one in Trepoldern could know in time. The sea had already washed almost to the cave mouth; little, gentle-looking waves, but nothing would stop them. That serene view seen through the opening might have belonged to a world they had never known. "I have to keep calm. I have to do something," Laura told herself.

But she was helplessly trussed against the wall of the cave.

The Cave of the Great Horse. The cave, legend had it, from which the horse had come. Laura thought of the tossing black thing, remembering the magic of the tune, the gaiety of the inhabitants of Trepoldern, as though it had happened very long ago. Only that morning . . . only—how long?—since the hairy young man had been shot. She had lost track of time, but at least an hour must have passed. Probably more.

A wave washed right into the cave.

"I tried to save the cups," she said. "I threw them into the gorse when you attacked him, Isaac. I wonder if he's noticed they're missing? It will delay him, if he guesses where they are. The bushes are close and prickly and they went well in."

"The sea's coming!" Lelant sobbed. The next wave had washed halfway across the sandy floor. "Oh, Laura, what shall we do?"

There seemed nothing they could do. They were hopelessly imprisoned in the Cave of the Great Horse, facing death from the rising water.

16. The End of May Day

When the shot came Elvan was alone in the crowd, well within sight of all that happened. He saw the hairy young man fall and Rose collapse into Peter's arms. For a moment, along with everyone else, he stood transfixed, then he saw Rose move and stand on her own feet, and knew she wasn't hurt.

It was then, as chaos broke out, that Elvan started to look for Laura. But he was jammed at the front of the curious, anxious mob, and Laura was at the very back, and he couldn't see her. He couldn't get back, so he went forward, and he was in time to see the extraordinary change in Mr. Summer's manner. He had straightened himself, so that suddenly he looked commanding, and his voice had a ringing quality, very different from his former fussy mumbling.

He bent over the young man and then ordered everyone to keep back.

"Who's he to give orders?" asked an old woman.

"Scotland Yard," said Mr. Summer. "You'll understand later. You!" to Elvan, who had now reached the front. "Stand here and keep them back. You help him, Mr. Poldern," to Peter. "I've got to get to a telephone. Where are those three policemen of yours? Oh, there they are. I'll send them through." And he strode away. The crowd, not getting it at all but unable to deny his air of command, parted to let him pass.

"But what—Scotland Yard? What the devil is it all about?" Peter asked. He had pushed Rose gently aside, and she stood with her hands tensely clasped, her face still very white.

On the cobblestones the hairy young man gave a faint groan. There was blood seeping through his dirty sweater and what they could see of his face through the hair was very white.

"He isn't dead!" said Elvan. "*I* don't know what happened. Where did the shot come from?"

The three young policemen had now come forward and formed a strong barrier. Their slow, good-humored faces looked bewildered. They parried the crowd's questions.

"Just got to wait," said P.C. Trelawney. "Just be patient, me dears. Ambulance coming."

"But who tried to kill him?"

The sun beat down, the sky was cloudless blue, and seagulls cried over the deserted boats in the harbor. Elvan stayed on by the injured man, but his eyes ranged the crowd. Where was Laura? Where were Lellie and Isaac?

In a very short time Mr. Summer was back.

"Got it in hand," he said. "I thought Arthur had gone

a couple of hours ago. I put out the alarm and all the roads have been watched since one o'clock. But seems he was here until a few minutes ago . . . . under the horse's trappings."

"Under the *horse?*"

"Yes, there's a bullet hole in the tarpaulin, and I've just met Mrs. Bailey. She found Billy Bailey and another man knocked out and trussed up in the loft. Our friend must have hidden there until it was time to start dancing. Mad as they come," he added grimly.

"Look, sir, I don't understand it," said Elvan. "But you say you're from Scotland Yard. We were on to something, but not clear about it. And I can't see Laura or the children. Laura and I were together until a few minutes before the shot, then we got separated. She *should* be here. I'm so afraid she saw something—"

Mr. Summer looked grimmer than ever and said something under his breath.

"Police from Bodmin and Launceston are closing in," he explained. "Can't have got far. Probably still here somewhere. What makes you think Laura would—?"

"I don't *know,*"Elvan answered, rather desperately. "It's just a feeling I have. Call it instinct. If she was near the hoss and saw what happened—"

"No one seemed to see," said Mr. Summer. "But come with me. She helped me a little, but I wish you'd all stayed out of it. I've told everyone I met to find Arthur Pengwern, but to be careful. He's armed and must be desperate now."

He went up the street almost a run, with Elvan at his

heels, and disappeared into the cottage that acted as a police station. In a moment he was back with a megaphone, and his strong voice roared over the lingering crowd, just as an ambulance swept up and was waved on to the scene of the accident.

"Keep calm, everyone. My name is Superintendent Bright of Scotland Yard. Arthur Poldern may still be in the town, and he is armed. If anyone has any information, please come to me. Is Laura Edmund anywhere around? Has anyone seen her, or Lelant and Isaac Tregarth?"

"I'm worried about the kids because Laura said they were sticking close to Arthur this morning," Elvan confessed. "We didn't know. . . . How *can* they have got on to anything? But they're not here. Oh, here's Father!"

George Tregarth came up rapidly.

"What an extraordinary business! What's it about? Scotland Yard—Bright—You were on the case of the Poldern Cups! I thought I knew your voice, but I didn't recognize. . . . Why do you want Laura and the children?"

"Because they're not here and they may be involved." Just as the superintendent spoke, a big young fisherman came running up.

"Sir! Sir!" he panted. "I went back to see if Grandma was all right. She's bedridden. Cottage on the corner of Oyster Passage and the lane up to Poldern Place. She says they all went up towards the Place. The children first, ten minutes before the others. Arthur Pengwern went by quickly, and she says he looked hot and furtive, then a young girl followed him, looking round the corner first. Grandma thought it very odd."

Superintendent Bright swore, and Elvan's heart seemed to turn over. The children, Laura and a madman with a gun!

"I'll phone the Place," said the Superintendent, and shot back into the police station. He came back, shaking his head.

"Mr. Mark Poldern answered. He's seen none of them."

"They must have gone to the Folly!" said Elvan.

Afterwards he never liked to remember the time that followed. A police car arrived in the town and orders were radioed to other cars. On Elvan's information, one was ordered to wait at the point where the path from the Folly emerged on the top lane.

Superintendent Bright, Elvan, and his father were driven up toward the Place in the police car, and they and the two policemen plunged into the woods. They approached the Folly quietly, gradually closing in, but it was soon clear that no one was there. The open stone told its own story, and so did clear footprints in the mud behind the Folly. The children and two adults had gone that way; and they found the place where Arthur's car might have been hidden. But the men waiting in the upper lane had seen nothing.

The two cars drove on to where the Bodmin and Poldern Head lanes forked and there they saw a man driving a red tractor in a field. He came over at once when he saw the cars and police, and said no, he hadn't bothered to go to the Festival. He wasn't a local and he'd sooner earn some money. He'd only seen one car go by and that was some time ago, when he'd been taking a rest in the hedge. A very old car, with a young man in a raincoat driving, a girl in front, and, he thought, two children in the back. They'd gone up to the Head and not, he was pretty sure, come back.

The cars were off before he had properly finished speaking.

"But why? Why?" asked Elvan.

"Anything up there?" asked Superintendent Bright.

"Only the cliffs and the cove. And a cave, but the tide will be up by now."

"Hurry!" George Tregarth urged the driver.

They found Arthur's old car abandoned on the cliff top, and Arthur himself lying dead near the bottom of the cliffpath. His hands and face were covered with terrible scratches, as though he had fought his way through gorse bushes, and his neck was broken.

"But Laura—the children . . ." cried Elvan, and scarcely paused to glance at Arthur. He only saw the cave mouth, with the sea already washing into it. He started off across the higher rocks, then plunged up to his shoulders in a deep hollow.

But he had heard voices, and a young, terrified scream. He was up on the next rock in a moment, struggling on. And then he saw Laura in the mouth of the cave, dragging Lelant. A wave washed over them.

Elvan was a strong swimmer and he was past the rocks. He put his head down and did a vigorous crawl stroke for some yards. When he looked up he saw Laura's face, white and wet. She was still holding Lelant, who seemed unconscious.

"Where's Isaac?" he gasped.

"Behind. I—I couldn't hold them both and he said he could swim. I only untied myself at the last minute. The rope was rotted."

"Can *you* swim?"

"A little. Not very well. I—" Then a strong wave almost washed Laura and Lelant back into the cave. As it receded Isaac appeared. He was swimming, white-faced but oddly composed.

Elvan knew his little brother was a fine swimmer for his age. He said: "Good boy, Isaac! Can you make for the rocks? I'll bring the others."

But how was he to rescue two? Especially when the tide only wanted to wash them against the cliff face or into the cave. In those moments Elvan was faced with the worst dilemma of his life. His little sister—or the girl who, he suddenly knew, had grown important.

Behind him there were shouts and then George Tregarth was there, seizing Lelant. Elvan took Laura and began to fight the tide. They all struggled to the highest rocks and were hauled, dripping, from the sea.

Three hours later the whole Tregarth family, Laura, and Superintendent Bright sat with the Polderns in the drawing room at Poldern Place. The superintendent looked very different from the man they had known as a folklorist, though he still wore his disreputable suit

The End of May Day   183

and shoes. But the straggling grey hair had gone, revealing a man of nearly sixty; sharp-faced, alert, and with short hair only just greying at the temples.

By then everyone knew most of the story. The cups had been found in the gorse bushes where Laura had thrown them. The hairy young man, in the hospital in Newquay and not expected to live, had nevertheless been able to talk. His name was Brian Blake and he really was Arthur Pengwern's stepbrother, only Arthur's real identity was Jack Penporth, son of the man who had committed that long-ago murder and robbery. The older Jack had taken his family to London, then to Australia, where, on the death of his wife, he had married again.

Superintendent Bright explained that he had never quite given up the Poldern case, and he had always suspected Jack Penporth. He had known when the family went to Australia, and then the case had really seemed to die. But it was well known at the Yard that he had never quite forgotten events in Trepoldern, and when a strange piece of news had come in he had been told at once. A half-dead young man had been picked up in Sidney Harbour. He was without identity papers, but he had been able to say, eventually, that he was Arthur Pengwern and that he had intended to fly to Britain the day after he was attacked, to get to know his grandparents in Trepoldern. But he had been set on by two men who had gotten acquainted with him and thrown him into the water, presumably dead. The Sydney police had discovered that someone calling himself

Arthur Pengwern had taken a plane for London.

At Superintendent Bright's request, the Australian police had investigated Jack Penporth and his family, and found that the father was hopelessly incapacitated. He had had two strokes some while before, and had just had a third one that might be fatal. His daughters were married and safely at home in Melbourne and Adelaide, but his son Jack and his stepson Brian had disappeared. Brian had flown out on another airline, his destination apparently France, but Superintendent Bright had assumed that the stepbrothers were both making for Trepoldern.

"So I decided on my charade," he had explained, as soon as he returned from the hospital where Brian Blake lay. "It seemed obvious then that Jack Penporth had hidden the cups twenty years ago and that the sons were on the way to find them. I've now heard most of the rest of the story. Brian is dying, but he was anxious to talk. He says that when their father had the second stroke he tried to tell them something, and they grasped that the Poldern cups were somewhere in Trepoldern. They'd already heard the story, but had no idea their father had been the thief and murderer. He seems only to have been able to get over to them that the cups were in a tower, and something about a swinging stone."

"I didn't know about the secret hiding place," said Mark Poldern. "But I remember that Jack Penporth worked up at the Folly for a while. Cleaning it up and seeing to the doors and windows. He must have found it then, but I think it was at least a year before the theft. I never gave the matter another thought."

"Well, the young men had a great piece of luck. A few weeks after hearing the story they learned that Arthur Pengwern planned to visit the Vicarage in Trepoldern. The Penporths lived in Sydney and Arthur was born there, but they'd never met. Arthur's maternal grand-parents took him to the Outback, and the Penporths heard through another family, with whom they'd kept in touch.

"Arthur was coming to Sydney and staying at a certain hotel before flying out. So they got to know him without telling him their real names, and found out all they could about his background. Then they lured him to the harbor on a dark night, and, as they thought, murdered him. But they were careless, and he wasn't dead when he was thrown into the water. Brian said Jack always resented his part in the affair, and Brian didn't trust Jack."

"We thought *you* were in it," said Laura. "We thought you were a very suspicious character."

Superintendent Bright laughed.

"You helped me quite a bit, putting me on to the towers. That time I met you in the tower on the North Cliff was just a coincidence. . . . I really was looking at the view. Old Jack's wife insisted she knew nothing. An unintelligent woman, and not, apparently, fond of her own son or Brian. We didn't think she'd try to warn them, but a watch has been kept on her. I'm afraid I took too many risks, but I was biding my time, because

I wanted the cups and I didn't want anything to alarm the stepbrothers. It seemed clear the two had no real idea where they were. I did have the Bodmin and Launceston police behind me, ready to go into action, but I only told the men here when I lost Arthur after the hoss had gone in this morning."

"Those poor old people at the Vicarage!" said Mrs. Tregarth. "One of us ought to go and see them."

"Well, they were pretty upset, though presumably the real Arthur will come when he's fully recovered. When I lost him and saw his car had gone, I went to the Vicarage, and he wasn't there. His clothes were gone, and Hannah found the note under his pillow." Superintendent Bright paused, looking at Elvan and Laura. "If I'd realized you'd really gotten yourselves involved I'd have warned you to keep away from it all."

"You knew the hairy young man was Brian? You were talking to him outside The Cornish Cream," said Elvan.

"I didn't *know,*" the Superintendent said. "But I was pretty sure. You probably never heard him speak, but he had an Australian accent."

"I did hear him speak," said Laura, with a shiver. "Down on the shore, when I first realized about the cups. And again at the inn last night, but we couldn't see who it was. I think he was playing 'Waltzing Matilda' once, on the cliff at night. That ought to have been a clue, as it's Australian."

"Actually I'd followed Arthur up the North Cliff that day he met Brian," Superintendent Bright explained. "I guessed he was up to something. I hid in the bushes and saw them both leave separately. You were luckier, you heard what they said."

"It's all been most unfortunate and dangerous," said George Tregarth. "When I think of you children—"

"It was awful!" said Lelant. "We'll never look for a mystery again. But Laura was wonderful. She saved us more than once."

"Yes, we owe a lot to Laura," said Mrs. Tregarth.

Laura caught the words and smiled, but she was only half-listening. She was remembering the moment when Elvan had helped her up the cliff path and called her "my dear" in a special voice. And she was thinking of Rose, who would be happy now. For she and Peter seemed to have come to some understanding.

"Without Laura we might not have saved the cups," said Mark Poldern. The two small, beautiful things were on a table beside him. Exquisitely wrought, gleaming, they seemed to embody long-ago times. They had not been damaged by their years in John Poldern's secret corner. Each had been wrapped in thick material and the leather bag had protected them.

"You might have anyway," said Laura. "All the roads were watched."

"It's possible," agreed the superintendent. "But he seems to have been desperate as well as unbalanced. He could have hidden them again, or been clever enough to get out of Cornwall with them."

"It's ruined May Day, of course," said George Tregarth.

"Not quite," said Mark Poldern. "Billy Bailey has to

188   The May Day Mystery

rest, but the hoss is coming out again this evening and we must all be there."

Yes, they must, thought Laura, remembering the hoss with a thrill. Perhaps she and Elvan would be together.

It was an enchanting evening, softly colored and still. At seven-thirty the hoss came out, bursting forth into the silent, waiting crowd. The people of Trepoldern were still stunned by the events of the afternoon, but there was after all only one May Day, and the hoss mattered. The music struck up and once more the ancient tune filled the narrow streets.

Rose and Peter walked hand in hand, and Laura was with Elvan as she had hoped. He did not hold her hand, but he was always close beside her as they followed the hoss around the town and down to the harbor.

"Sing, sing, for summer now is come—"

Living and dying. . . . the music grew louder as May Day moved toward its end. Everyone in the town was singing; the rhythm seemed as if it would never stop. But, at last, the hoss turned back toward the Great Horse Inn. It died for the last time outside the ancient door, then lived again to move around to the yard in front of the loft. By then it was growing dark and the moon rode high.

Laura wondered, as the last verse rang out, if she would ever hear the tune again.

"—And luck be with you on May Day!"

Well, in a way luck had certainly been with her. She and the children might be dead now in the cave.

Then the hoss had gone and it was all over. Or so

Laura thought until Elvan took her hand and drew her away from the crowd, down to the almost deserted harbor. They walked far along the South Quay and sat on an upturned boat, and then Elvan put his arm around Laura and drew her to him. He kissed her slowly and warmly and Laura responded with her whole heart. They had not known each other long, but on her part it had been love at first sight . . . or even, perhaps, when she had first seen his photograph.

"Oh, Laura!" said Elvan, when he released her. "I never thought when Rose said she was bringing a friend for May Day that you'd turn out to be important. The most important thing that's ever happened to me. I know we've only known each other for a while. . . . I know you're pretty young. But—"

"I shall have to go away, back to London," Laura whispered.

"But you'll come back. Rose says you have another week's vacation later. You must come then. I'll be here waiting for you, so come as soon as you can."

"But—"

"I want you to marry me. How would you feel about that?"

"I—Yes," said Laura. "But I'd have to tell my parents. They're out of England."

"Oh, of course. They must come down, too, when they get back from Africa. We won't hurry things too much. Rose, I think, won't go back to London."

"I'm so glad it's worked out well for her," said Laura. "But I'll miss her."

"She'll be your sister-in-law by next year," said Elvan.

They walked slowly back to the castle. Behind them in the town there were still snatches of the May Song. Laura would never have believed she could be so happy. She would see other May Days, and perhaps, even, her children would be introduced to the Great Horse.